Thomas William Robertson, Victorien Sardou

Progress!

A Comedy

Thomas William Robertson, Victorien Sardou

Progress!
A Comedy

ISBN/EAN: 9783744784764

Printed in Europe, USA, Canada, Australia, Japan

Cover: Foto ©Andreas Hilbeck / pixelio.de

More available books at **www.hansebooks.com**

PROGRESS!

A Comedy,

(FOUNDED ON "LES GANACHES," BY VICTORIEN SARDOU).

BY

T. W. ROBERTSON.

___ ___

CHARACTERS.

LORD MOMPESSON.	JOHN FERNE.
The HON. ARTHUR MOMPESSON.	MR. DANBY.
DR. BROWN.	WYKEHAM.
MR. BUNNYTHORNE.	EVA.
BOB BUNNYTHORNE.	MISS MYRNIE.

SCENE.—*Mompesson Abbey.*

A lapse of two months between the First and Second Acts. A lapse of one night between the Second and Third.

ACT I.

SCENE I.—*Drawing-room in Mompesson Abbey. Door* C. *Small door* R. *Old-fashioned large fire-place* R. *Scene enclosed. Window* L. (*See* diagram.) *Outside window, garden and park seen. The trees covered with snow. Large fire burning. Pictures on walls, &c. Sofas, chairs, couches, tables, all old-fashioned. An air of great antiquity, and tumble-down comfort about everything. Vestiges of feudalism ranged here and there.*

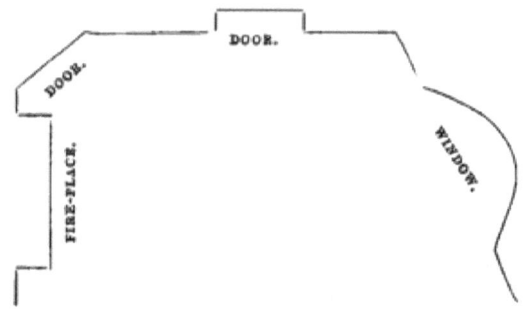

Enter DANBY *and* FERNE, *conducted by* WYKEHAM, C. D. FERNE *carries a portfolio.*

WYK. (*An old servant, of about* 66.) If you'll be good enough to sit down, gentlemen, Mr. Arthur will see you directly.

[*Exit* WYKEHAM, C. D.

FER. A fire—a lovely fire. My fingers are almost frozen.

DAN. So odd that I should find you sketching and planning as I drove past. It's more than two years since we met.

FER. I was going to call here when I'd finished my plan. I have business with Lord Mompesson.

DAN. With old Lord Mompesson? You'll find it difficult to transact business with him.

FER. Why?

DAN. He never attends to business. He's too old.

FER. Too old! A man of fifty?

DAN. Fifty! Why, he's over eighty!

FER. What! is not the old lord dead yet?

DAN. No. I suppose you're thinking of his only son, the Honourable Arthur. Do you know him?

FER. I did some years ago.

DAN. How was that?

FER. My grandfather was a tenant.

DAN. Oh, yes; I remember. Before '32?

FER. Yes. They quarrelled with my father about his vote on that occasion. My father left the farm.

DAN. And took to scientific drainage; lucky for you, for thanks to that, here you are, at thirty years of age, a rising engineer, making a fortune and a name.

FER. Never mind that. Tell me about the Mompesson family. But, first, how is it I find you here?

DAN. Don't you know? Since my father-in-law retired from practice I'm the family lawyer.

FER. And the old lord is still living?

DAN. Yes,—that is, he lives a little, preparatory to dying a great deal.

FER. He was a very old man when I was quite a boy.

DAN. Of course! You know the story, don't you? The old lord—always a poor man—had hopes for his son in Parliament, so in '29 he bought a rotten borough—Wapshot-cum-Chuddock.

FER. Which in '32 was disfranchised.

DAN. Just so—and the family was ruined. However, there was but one son—this Arthur—who at that time was in the Guards, a fine, handsome, young officer. Well, father and son took this misfortune so to heart that young Arthur left the army, and, with his father, settled down here in the old Abbey, on their own estate, near Stickton-le-Clay, and have given no attention to politics or public life ever since. This, they say, is a degenerate, peddling age, and they will have none of it; they have cut the world—a slight of which the world is quite unconscious.

FER. And what sort of a man has the Honourable Arthur crusted into?

DAN. A country gentleman of the old school. Urbane, refined, polished, and prejudiced. A great man at Quarter Sessions—and at the County Ball. A crystallized Quixote, doing battle with everything new.

Fer. Is he clever?

Dan. He has a gentlemanly intellect, somewhat narrow-minded—and large-hearted. He is a noble fellow despite his prejudices. High-minded, chivalric, brave, and courteous. He would have made a splendid crusader, if he'd had the ill-luck to have been born six hundred years ago. Chop him into mincemeat, and every atom would be gentleman.

Fer. And such a man can shut himself up in this hole of a village!

Dan. With his father—to whom he is devoted. He has also another attached friend, who almost lives in the house. One Dr. Brown—a most amusing inconsistency—moral, political, and medical. A radical—a chartist—a republican of the reddest dye; a materialist of the old French revolutionary type; an adorer of Cromwell, Voltaire, Robespierre, and William Cobbett; a man who wants to root up thrones and pull down churches—behead kings and burn clergymen—in the cause of order, law, liberty, equality, and fraternity. But with all this old-world folly the Doctor is an excellent man; high-minded and straightforward; a most skilful physician; indeed, it is he who keeps the old lord alive.

Fer. But how does the Doctor—this acid of radicalism, agree in the same house with the alkali of aristocracy?

Dan. Meaning the Honourable Arthur? Admirably. They used to hate each other, but when Arthur Mompesson fell from his horse in the hunting-field and broke his leg, the Doctor attended him, and, ever since, their personal attachment has been equal to their political antagonism. They discuss and quarrel over their wine. Let me tell you the Doctor is a teetotaller. Oh! how they discuss. Then there are two other people here, quite characters.

Fer. Who are they?

Dan. Old Bunnythorne, a retired contractor:—supplied provisions for the Navy; his father made a fortune at Portsmouth during the war.

Fer. And what is he like?

Dan. Oh! he too grumbles at everything new, and growls a perpetual chorus of compliments to the good old times. Not that he has much cause to grumble. Oh, yes! I forgot. He has one.

Fer. What's that?

Dan. His son,—his only son,—Bob, a conceited young lout who, because his father won't give him money to go up to London to waste his time and health there, gets drunk at the

"Mompesson Arms" here every night in the society of Miss Brill the barmaid and one Jack Topham, a man much looked up to in these parts by ostlers and stable-boys. Bob, too, considers himself quite a literary character.

Fer. Why ?

Dan. I don't know. I suppose because he can't spell properly, or because he's thoroughly impracticable, and never understands the poetry he reads.

Fer. A very singular family group. And are there no women in the house ?

Dan. Yes, two. One a Miss Myrnie, a detestable old maid,—scandal-loving, mischief-making, snuff-taking, poodle-doggy, and generally disagreeable. She is some sixteenth cousin, and remains here out of ——

Fer. Charity ?

Dan. No;—kinsmanship. She has, perhaps, five drops of the Mompesson blood in her, and that is quite enough for my lord and for his son.

Fer. And the other lady ?

Dan. Oh ! a girl of 18,—also some distant cousin. I don't know much about her, except that her mother made some *mésalliance*, and married a man in business. The father and mother dying, the girl was received here. I have been told that at first neither my lord nor his son cared much about her presence, they were so indignant at her mother's conduct, but now they are both very much attached to her. Poor girl ! she has been very ill, and is only just recovering.

Fer. (*Looking at his watch.*) Time that I should go, and so I must leave my card (*leaves card in basket*), and call again when I am here in two months' time.

Dan. Won't you drive back with me and dine ?

Fer. Impossible. I must finish my plan, and sleep in London to-morrow night, to meet the Board the next morning. (*Going.*)

Dan. Well, good bye. Stop ! You're doing well, and making your fortune. Why don't you get married ?

Fer. (*Smiling.*) Married ! I never have the time. You must meet a girl at least three or four times before you propose to her, and what with one thing and the other——

Dan. Have you never met anyone who——

Fer. Well—yes,—(*reflecting*)—I did think : but no, it was nothing. (*Looking at watch.*) Matrimony doesn't go well with engineering, so I must die a bachelor. (*Looks at watch.*) Good bye !

DAN. (*Shaking hands.*) Goodbye. (*Exit* FERNE, C. D.) How that young fellow has got on since I first knew him; but no wonder—clever, sober, industrious——

Enter BOB, *followed by* WYKEHAM, C. D.

DAN. (*Seeing him.*) Ah! this is quite another sort of thing.

WYKE. Really, sir, you must not smoke anywhere but in the smoking-room : my lord don't like it.

BOB. Old fool!

WYKE. Mr. Arthur don't like it.

BOB. Old fool!

WYKE. And your father don't like it, sir.

BOB. Another old fool! There! (*putting up his pipe in case*) that's gone out, and now you can go out! (*Exit* WYKEHAM.) Another old fool! Everybody here 's an old fool—except me. Eh! Danby, is that you? I thought it was my guv'nor.

DAN I have not the good fortune to be your guv'nor.

BOB. You're lucky ?

DAN. I think so.

> [BOB *to be got up like the conventional poet; but dirty and slovenly, velvet coat, long black hair, pale face, spectacles, a sort of pot-house Manfred.*]

BOB. My father's as much behind the age as I am above these wretched, stupid surroundings. I rust here—rust—regularly rust. I'm like a bright sword steeped in ditch-water.

DAN. (*Aside*). More like a soft spoon steeped in beer.

BOB. (*Spouting*)—

> " My thoughts from 'mid the vulgar herd gyrate from pole to pole ;
> Patience, my heart, oh rest, my brain, oh wait, my weary soul!"

Did you ever read my poems ? My " Thoughts in a Crater ?"

DAN. No.

BOB. I'll lend 'em to you. They're in manuscript.

DAN. (*Quickly*). Thanks. I have no time.

BOB. The guv'nor won't let me publish. He won't give me the money. Could you lend me a sovereign ?

DAN. I'd rather not, if it's all the same to you.

Bob. Like the rest of 'em! O world! world! (*Spouts.*)

" Patience, my heart, oh rest, my brain, oh wait, my weary soul!"

Dan. Why not thirsty soul?

Bob. Danby. To the calm and dispassionate observer it is curious to think what an infernal old fool my father is! If my poems were published in London, I should realize a fortune; then, with his capital, I could start a new magazine or a daily newspaper!

Dan. And does he refuse to indulge you to that trifling extent?

Bob. He does! Oh, these fathers! what misfortunes they are to men of genius.

Bun. (*Without.*) The horse is right enough—never mind the horse! Look after me! I think I've broken something somewhere!

Bob. There he is!

Enter Bunnythorne, c.d., *his hat smashed; hat and coat covered with snow.*

Bun. (*As he enters.*) Send for the doctor!

Dan. } What is the matter?

Bob. } What's happened, guv'nor?

Bun. I was driving back—everything was white with snow —and, I suppose, I got off the road into the ditch. Down we went—and then on one side—b-r-r-r-r. What weather! There never used to be any snow in the winter when I was a young man!

Bob. No snow?

Bun. At least, if there was, the snow wasn't cold, and it never filled up the ditches. Everything has degenerated, even the snow!

Bob. Guv'nor, the fact is, if you don't know how to drive, you should get somebody to drive you.

Bun. Hold your tongue! It was that beast of a horse; but there are no horses now-a-days! No beasts worth their straw!

Bob. No beasts?

Bun. Except you! Why didn't you come home last night?

Bob. I slept at Jack Topham's.

Bun. Jack Topham's! A nice acquaintance for a young man of fortune!

Bob. Pretty fortune! Ten bob a week for pocket-money!

Bun. With your prospects!

Bob. Pretty prospects! Stickton-le-Clay and its neighbourhood!

Bun. Hold your tongue!

Bob. Can't I speak?

Bun. No! Not when your father's been thrown out of a gig!

Bob. I wish to console you.

Bun. Console—humbug! Hold your tongue!

Bob. I shan't!

> *Enter* Dr. Brown. *Blue coat, brass buttons, dark drab breeches and gaiters, all loose and easy, spotlessly clean; very loose large white neckerchief; red healthy face; a homely grandeur about the man; long white hair flowing over the coat collar.*

Doc. Now, what's all this fuss about?

Bob. The guv'nor's spilt himself.

Bun. I didn't—it was the gig. The gigs never used to spill in my time.

Doc. (*Feeling his arms, &c.*) Stand up. Move your arms —so.

Bob. (*To* Danby.) The gig spilt him,—reasonable, isn't it? Nice lot of old fools I'm condemned to waste my burning youth among.

Doc. You're all right. (*To* Bunnythorne.) Perhaps a bruise or two. I'll make you up an embrocation.

Bob. You're not hurt. (*Spouts.*)

" For the linnet loves its egglets ere a feather deck their wings;
   And the love-birds peck their mother, as their lullaby she sings."

Doc. What, ain't you dead yet? (*To* Bob.)

Bob. Doctor!

Doc. At the rate you're going it, I give you eighteen months longer. You're as white as a sheet. Look at your liver, sir! —look at it! I should like you to see your own liver.

Bun. I shouldn't.

Bob. Really, if I'm treated in this way, I'll go——

Bun. Do—do—and don't come back.

Bob. Such language to your own son——

Doc. Pooh! Parentage is a mere accident.

Bun. Accident! In this case it's an offence.

Bob. Of all the ignorance——

Enter the HON. ARTHUR MOMPESSON, C. D. (*Morning dress of the late Duke of Wellington, blue frock coat, buff waistcoat, black stock, grey trousers, grey hair.*)

ART. Good morning, my dear Mr. Danby. I fear I've kept you waiting.

DAN. I have some leases that want renewing, and a few other papers to submit to Lord Mompesson.

ART. He will be here directly. Bunnythorne, I hear you've had a bad fall.

BUN. All falls are bad now-a-days. Augh! I've no patience. When I used to fall, thirty years ago, I didn't feel it half so much.

BOB. You were younger then.

BUN. I was not. (*In a passion.*) Don't talk to me.

DOC. Don't excite yourself. You'll bruise your—intellect.

BOB. He won't feel it in that quarter. (*Aside.*)

Enter MISS MYRNIE, C. D. (*an old maid of 53, rusty black silk, and mortified manner of a pew-opener.*) *She carries in her arms a little lap-dog.*

MISS MYR. (*Carneying.*) Good morning, dear Mr. Arthur. I was not down soon enough to meet you at breakfast. (*To dog.*) Wish Mr Arthur good morning, Pamela. Dear Mr. Bunnythorne, how do you do?

BUN. Black and blue all over.

MISS MYR. And dear Robert, too. (BOB *nods sulkily.*) And the Doctor. (*Aside.*) An irreligious wretch. (*To dog.*) Never mind him, Pamela; he shall not harm us.

ARTHUR *and* DANBY *talking near fire-place* R. BOB *seated* R. BUNNYTHORNE *and* DOCTOR L.

Oh, Mr. Bunnythorne, here's your newspaper. (*Giving it.*)

BUN. (*Unfolding paper.*) And a pretty thing a newspaper is now-a-days. Why, they sell some of 'em for a penny. Nice news they must contain for a penny!

DOC. Ay, indeed; Cobbett's Weekly Register——

BUN. Bother Cobbett!

DOC. Don't abuse Cobbett.

ART. Why not? He abused everybody.

Doc. You must not touch giants. Respect the ashes of the great Cobbett, and of Cromwell, and——

Art. Cromwell—a butcher!

Bun. No; a brewer.

Dan. (*Aside*). Now they've begun.

Bun. I always liked Cromwell.

Doc. Why?

Bun. Because he *was* a brewer.

Art. And rose from his malt-tubs to usurp a throne. A regicide!

Doc. That was his great merit. He taught indignant peoples to kill kings.

Miss M. Listen to him, Pamela, and bite him when he's not looking. (*To* dog.)

Doc. The three great epochs of modern times were '89, '32, and '48; since then the world has ceased to move. Cromwell showed the French the way to deal with despots.

Bob. I don't think much of Cromwell.

Doc. *You* don't think much of Cromwell? You! I wonder what Cromwell would have thought of you.

Bob. His killing of Charles——

Art. Assassination!

Doc.] Righteous execution! } *together.*
Art.] Infamous assassination!}

Bob. His suppression of his breathing apparatus. There! Cromwell was only an imitator; Brutus killed Cæsar in the capitol long ago.

Bun. In the good old times!

Doc. What the devil——

Art. (*Pointing to* Miss Myrine). Hush! hush!

Bun. (*Who has been reading paper*) Another railway accident. Go it! go it! nineteenth century!

Art. Not a fatal accident, I hope.

Bun. One woman killed!

Doc. Only a woman!

Miss M. Only a woman!

Doc. I meant only *one* woman.

Art. Are you disappointed that a dozen were not sacrificed to this modern scientific apparatus for swift slaughter?

Doc. Woman, considered from the point of view of reason, is an inferior animal to man.

Miss M. The villain! (*To* Dog). You hear what he says of us, my dear?

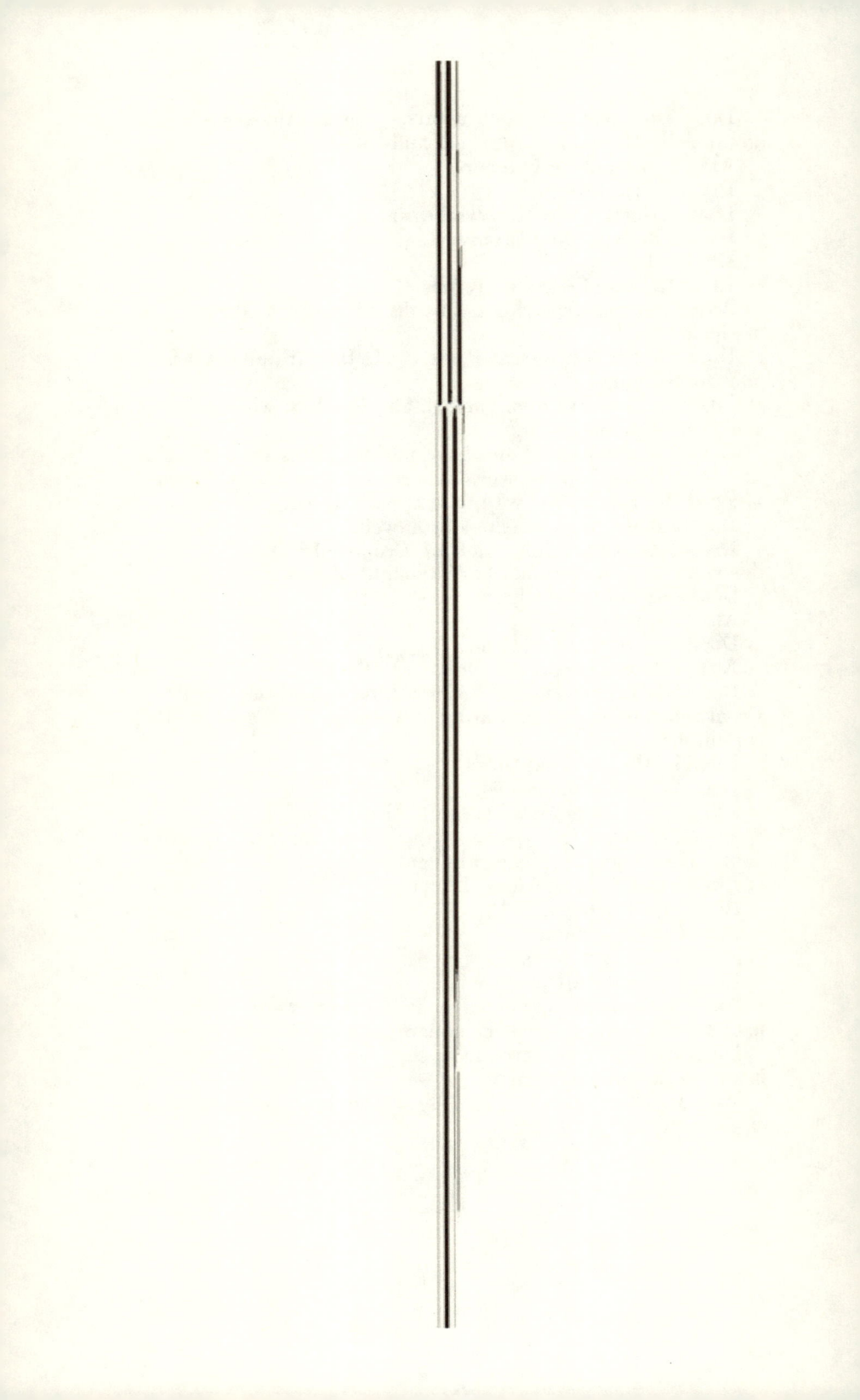

Doc. Anatomy proves it.

Art. Anatomy! What has the mutilation and desecration of the dead to do with the beauty of a life? What has the grace, charm, goodness, heroism, patience, the *mind*, the soul, to do with anatomy?

Doc. Nothing whatever. I speak as a materialist. Woman——

Miss M. (*Rising*). Doctor, if you are going to use bad language we will retire.

Doc. Miss Myrnie, when I said woman I meant nothing personal to you. (Miss Myrnie, *appeased, sits down again; the* c. *door is opened by* Wykeham, Lord Mompesson *led by* Eva *enters.*

       [Lord Mompesson, *an old man of* 80, *in a dressing-gown and skull-cap.*

Lord M. Good morning, good folks, good morning. Mr. Danby, how do you do? Excuse me for having kept you waiting. Arthur have you made my excuses to Mr. Danby? My good Doctor, you don't know how much I am indebted to my good nurse. She's been reading to me this morning. She is quite my *gouvernante.*

Miss M. Good morning, my lord! (*To* Eva). Good morning, dear! (*Aside*). He never asks me to read to him. Ah, (*To* dog) Pamela, we have none of the beauty of the serpent when the serpent's an egg!

Dr. Miss Eva is the best nurse in the world.

Lord M. Why—why—why did you not come here sooner, Eva? You've not been here—no, not twelve months; and we're all in love with you, ar'nt we, eh?

Miss M. (*Aside*). I'm not in love with her. Ah, these men! They never will understand women!

Eva. Oh! Don't talk in that way. You'll make me so vain! You'll spoil me!

Bun. (*To* Bob). Go and talk to her. If you are a poet, behave as such.   [Bob *gets near to* Eva. R.H.

Art. Mr. Danby has some business—if you could see him. (*To* Lord Mompesson).

Bob. (*Aside*). She is not a patch upon Miss Brill at the "Arms." (*To* Eva). Eva, you've never read my poems?

Eva. No; I've been so well lately, and the weather's been so fine.

Bob. Then you don't know my lines—— (*Spouting*)

" When the white-winged wind woos winter, and the robin flees the wold,
And the lover leaves his lyre lest his fire turn to cold."

Pretty lines, ar'nt they ?

Eva. Very. What do they mean ?

Lord M. Mr. Danby, come with me. Come into my room.

Art. Shall I——

Lord M. No, no. When we want you we'll send for you.
(Arthur *opens door.* Danby *offers his arm to* Lord Mompesson.
They both go out. c.d.)

Bob. (*Pursuing* Eva)—

" For the Mayflies live in summer, though their life last but a day :
And the summer of a lover is as one eternal May."

Eva. (*Turning over card-basket*). This young man always
smells so dreadfully of tobacco. (*Sees* Ferne's *card, starts*) Oh !

Art. What's the matter ?

Eva. Nothing. (*Aside*). Has he been here ?

Bun. Pretty couple, ar'nt they ?

Miss M. I don't know. I never recognize couples. I consider them improper.

Doc. Why so ? There's you and Pamela.

Art. I don't consider Bob pretty.

Bun. But he will be—he will be. I was just the same at
his age.

Art. That hardly reassures me. But what do you mean ?

Bun. I mean,—why not marry them ?

Art.
Miss. M. } (*Astounded.*) What ?
Doc.

Bun. Make 'em man and wife. Bob would turn steady,
and——

Miss M. I don't like marriages, unless they are contracted
in a Christian spirit.

Art. (*His pride wounded.*) A member of my family.

Bun. Exactly ! Family on your side, money on mine.

Art. Money.

Eva. Can he have been here ? (*Aside.*)

Doc. Pooh ! Pooh ! Eva can't marry.

Art.
Miss M. } Certainly not !

Bun. Why not?

Doc. Why not? She is hardly convalescent. She has not entirely got over her last illness. Look at her now;—her eyes dilated; the nostrils distended; the short, catchy breathing,—all signs of poor, thin, weak, bad blood.

Art. Bad blood! My cousin!

Bun. We Bunnythornes have always had good, rich blood! Look at the spots on Bob's face.

Art. ⎱ The blood of the Mompessons! ⎱ (*Together.*)
Bun. ⎰ The blood of the Bunnythornes! ⎰

Doc. Blood! What *is* blood? (*Contemptuously.*)

Bun. ⎧ Oh! don't begin——
Art. ⎩ For goodness' sake—— ⎱ (*Together.*)
Miss M. Never mind them, Pamela! ⎰
Bob. ⎱ (*Spouting.*) " When the watch-
         dog barks his welcome." ⎰

Enter Wykeham, c. d.

Wyk. Lunch is on the table, sir.

Art. I have lunched.

Bun. I have not;—but I will. (*Rising.*)

Miss M. So will I. (*Rising.*)

Doc. And I. (*Rising.*)

Bob. Eva!—may I——

Eva. (*Thinking of card.*) No, thanks, I never lunch.

Bob. Nor I. I've no appetite.

Doc. I should think not, the life you lead. Go back to the public-house.

Bun. Leave the boy alone; you're always at him.

Doc. So are you.

Bun. But I'm his father.

Bob. And I wish you weren't. (*Spouts.*)

" Patience, my heart, oh rest, my brain, oh wait, my weary soul!"

Miss M. A set of brutes!

[*Exeunt all but* Eva *and* Arthur, c. d.

Eva r, Arthur l.

Eva. How could that card find its way here?

Art. (*Looking at her.*) 19,—19 from 50; 9 from 10, 1; 2 from 53,——31; 31 years. It's a long time to look forward to, but a short time to look back on. I feel as young as ever,

—younger; for I can appreciate the love of a good woman, as no lad of 20 knows how. (*Mournfully.*) Perhaps because I can no longer inspire it. A wasted life. A wasted life! And Arthur Mompesson, the dandy Guardsman, has sunk into an old bachelor with a talent for whist. Augh! (*Sighs*) That cub Bob! Old Bunnythorne to dare to—— Why not? Bob is her own age. Oh, youth! youth! To think that Bob should be so young and I should be so old. (*Crossing to* R.) Eva! (*Eva starts.*) What are you thinking of?

Eva. (*Placing card in basket.*) Thinking of—nothing.

Art. Why, your eyes are quite animated; and there is a flush on your cheek that gives you an expression as of a rose surprised.

Eva. Oh, cousin, you're very complimentary!

Art. Has anything happened?

Eva. No!

Art. You are looking much better these last few weeks.

Eva. Yes; I think my illness has passed. Everybody was very kind to me—you especially.

Art. And are you really happy with us?

Eva. Very happy!

Art. And have no regrets—no thoughts of those you have left?

Eva. Oh, yes! I sometimes think of them. They were very good people.

Art. Very good sort of people, no doubt, for tradespeople.

Eva. But tradespeople are as good as anybody else?

Art. Humph! (*Doubtfully.*)

Eva. You know papa died so suddenly that he left mamma very poor; and as mamma was not noticed by her family, she was forced to work.

Art. (*Aside.*) A Mompesson work!

Eva. And the Dobbses took a great deal of notice of her.

Art. The Magasin des Modes people?

Eva. Yes; and were very kind to her and to me, and paid my doctor's bill, and waited on me. Oh! so tenderly!

Art. No doubt the Dobbses are very good people, and must have expended a considerable sum of money on your account. I'll write to them to thank them, and enclose them a cheque for a hundred pounds. I suppose that will be enough?

Eva. Oh, you mustn't do that!

Art. Why not?

Eva. You'd offend them! The Dobbses are very proud.

ART. Oh, the Hobbses are proud, are they ? To think that pride could find a residence among the Hobbses.

EVA. Not Hobbses—Dobbses.

ART. Dobbses ?

EVA. They are truly noble people !

ART. Noble?

EVA. Not by descent, but feeling.

ART. Feeling ?

EVA. Heart !

ART. Heart ? Then you think that the qualities of the heart level all distinctions ?

EVA. I do.

ART. *All* distinctions?

EVA. Yes !

ART. Rank—birth ?

EVA. Yes !

ART. Genius—talent—wealth ?

EVA. Yes !

ART. Age ?—youth ? (*Changing his voice.*)

EVA. Yes ! (*A pause.*) Youth and age are only accidents. If one is good and kind and tender, what does it matter in what year one was born?

ART. (*Quickly.*) Not a bit !—not a bit ! I like the liberality of your sentiments, and—and—if—if—a—a man—or a woman I should say girl—were to fall in love—with—with—each other—the question of age need not ——

Enter WYKEHAM, C. D.

WYK. My lord wishes to see you for a few minutes.

ART. Yes. I'll come—I——. Excuse me, cousin (*Taking her hand.*) I was just going to say something which——. I'll be back directly. [*Exeunt* ARTHUR and WYKEHAM, C. D.

EVA. I cannot help wondering how that card came here. He must have called; and if he called he must——(*Looking into card-basket.*) (*Miss* MYRNIE *opens the little door* R. *and watches* EVA.) The card looks quite new. (*Going to window.*) It's more than a year now since I saw him. (*At window starts.*) Why, there he is, sketching! No ! I'm right ! it is he ! (*Trying to open window.*) Oh, these nasty old windows. (*Opens window and beckons.*) He doesn't see me. I'll send to him. Now he sees me ! Here—here ! Go round there to the left—to the door. How d'ye do ? how d'ye do ? I am so glad to see you.

(Coughs and places her hand on her chest, then shuts window.)
Oh, the cold air. I've not recovered yet.

Enter FERNE, C. D. MISS MYRNIE *closes door*, R.

FER. Somebody certainly beckoned me in. *(Seeing* EVA.*)*
Eh, Eva! you here?

EVA. Yes, me. Didn't you see me at the window?

FER. Was that you?

EVA. But why did you not come in without waiting to be asked. My uncle, Lord Mompesson, would be very glad to see you.

FER. Your uncle, Lord——

EVA. My grand-uncle.

FER. Lord Mompesson?

EVA. Yes. My mother's uncle. Since I saw you in London I've come to live with them.

FER. You surprise me! I knew that your mamma was of good family, but not——

EVA. I've been here eight months, and they're all so kind to me. How are the Dobbses?

FER. The Dobbses? I haven't seen them since I last saw you there. I've been abroad.

EVA. Where?

FER. In Russia principally.

EVA. Engineering?

FER. Engineering.

EVA. I had a letter from Mrs. Dobbs last week. I saw your card there just now. So kind of you to call and see me.

FER. To call and see you. *(Aside.)* She will have it I came to see her; though I did not know she lived here.

EVA. How came you to be in this neighbourhood?

FER. Eh? oh, business! *(Aside.)* I came to knock the house down.

EVA. However, I must present you to my uncle; then you can call when you please. Oh! I forgot! just now he's engaged with Mr. Danby.

FER. Mr. Danby?

EVA. Yes. Do you know him?

FER. I called here with him this morning.

EVA. Oh! you called with *him!*

FER. Yes. How well you're looking. Do you remember at the Dobbses when I used to call and see you, and you

sat in that big old armchair, by the fireside, propped up by pillows?

EVA. Oh, yes!—yes! That was a nice time!

FER. But now the colour has returned to your cheeks.

EVA. Come with me, and I'll show you over the Abbey, and by that time my uncle will be disengaged. (*Crossing* to L.

FER. But——

EVA. It's a wonderful place, the Abbey, one of the oldest in the kingdom. There are secret staircases and walls, and places I shudder as I pass, and down below—I've never been there, I'm too frightened—there are dungeons and cells, where, they say, poor people were shut up and tortured. Oh, horrible! is it not? (*Lowering her voice.*) Skeletons of the victims have been found within the last three years, and beneath where we are now standing is a crypt, in which are niches where living women were walled up alive, and left to die in the dark of thirst and hunger. (*Frightening herself with the recital.*) I cannot understand. The rulers of those days were good men, holy abbots, and pious pastors. Why were they so cruel? Thumbscrews, racks, dungeons, and burning stakes. Why—why—why did they brick up breathing, living women?

HIX. Because—because they lived in the good old times.

[*Exeunt* FERNE and EVA, C. D.

Miss MYRNIE *opens little door*, R.

MISS M. Oh, dear me!—oh, dear me! This is very bad!—this is very bad! I never see a young man and a young woman together but I suspect they care for each other. The wretches! And that Arthur! Oh, that Arthur! I know he's fond of the girl. Old fool! Why can't he seek a wife among his own connections—a woman of his own time of life—of ripe experience—mature charms, and pious feeling. A blessing on the heavenly side of 40; but, no! Mr. Arthur likes youth, and a slim waist, and a child's complexion, and baby tattle about ribbons and rubbish. But men are like that. The idiots! It is so ridiculous, the fuss they make in praise of youth. Why, everybody's had it once, and nobody can keep it long. Then it is so perishable. Youth soon fades away, but age lasts us to the latest hour.

Enter ARTHUR, C. D., *quickly*.

Art. Now, Eva, as I was —— (*Sees* Miss Myrnie—*disappointed.*) Oh! it is you, is it?

Miss M. Yes; I take that liberty. Did you expect to find Eva?

Art. (l.) Yes.

Miss M. (r.) She's not here.

Art. Where is she?

Miss M. She is showing the Abbey to a young gentleman.

Art. A young gentleman! Bob?

Miss M. No, not Bob. Ah! (*Sighing*). Would it were Bob!

Art. Eh, why?

Miss M. The young man is a stranger.

Art. A stranger!

Miss M. A perfect stranger. She saw him at that window. He made signs to her, and she made signs to him. Then she opened the window and beckoned him to come in, and he came in.

Art. (*Astonished*). Impossible! How came you to know all this?

Miss M. I saw them from behind that door.

Art. Then you were watching—listening.

Miss M. Heaven forbid! I hope I know my duty better. But—sometimes—one happens to open a door—by accident—when something is happening by accident, which we see by accident; or, one is behind a door by accident, and one hears something—entirely by accident and accidentally. It's happened to me often.

Art. But to speak to a stranger from a window!

Miss M. (*Crossing and closing window*). Why the sash is still open! I thought there was a draught.

Art. I can't believe it! Eva, so good—so truthful!

Miss M. So she is; that's what I always say.

Art. To accuse her——

Miss M. Accuse her! heaven forbid; Christian charity forbids that I should accuse anyone. I'm defending her.

Art. Defending her?

Miss M. Yes; she can't help it.

Art. Can't help——

Miss M. Running after a young man—after a *young* man —no—it's in her blood.

Art. In her blood?

Miss M. Yes; do you not remember twenty-four years ago, when her mother ran away with that low plebeian fellow Summers? It was at this very window that they used to

meet (ARTHUR *sinks in chair*) Romeo and Juliet over again; and it was like that villain Shakspeare to put it in a play.

ART. (*Rising*). Do me the favour to ask the Doctor and Mr. Bunnythorne to come here.

MISS M. With pleasure. As to dear Eva, I'm sure she's innocence itself. So youthful, so truthful—there's the pity. Innocence and youth are so apt to betray us, ain't they? But as I often tell tell my Pamela, she's a darling girl. Bless her! Bless her! Bless her!

Exit MISS MYRNIE, C. D.

ART. Eva beckon to a strange young man? Impossible! She must have known him. Some intrusive shop-boy from those people she was with—the—the Nobbses. A 'prentice! I—I— I—— At this very window, too, where her mother——it would seem as if there were a fate in it.

Enter DOCTOR *and* BUNNYTHORNE. BUNNYTHORNE *in nightcap and dressing-gown,* C. D.

DOC. Arthur, you sent for us.

BUN. The Doctor was sending me to bed, so I came as I am.

ART. I wanted your advice. I find that there is a young man here—a stranger—come after Eva.

DOC. } (*Together*). { Eva!
BUN. }

ART. Now should his intentions be matrimonial——

BUN. Matrimonial! Then what's to become of my boy Bob?

ART. (*Out of patience.*) Bob! You can't think of Eva and Bob.

BUN. Why not? They're both young.

ART. Eva is too young.

DOC. And too delicate.

BUN. Well, Bob's delicate, too.

ART. But a stranger coming here without introduction, and *sans ceremonie*——

DOC. Insolent!

BUN. Kick him out!

EVA *and* FERNE *appear at* C. *door,* ARTHUR, BUNNY-THORNE *and* DOCTOR *with their backs to the*

audience, MISS MYRNIE *at* C. *door. A pause, during which* MISS MYRNIE *crosses at back to door* R., *and goes off.*

EVA. (*Somewhat surprised at their aggressive attitude.*) Cousin, let me present——

ART. Not now. Your uncle wishes to see you upstairs.

EVA. But before——

ART. Don't keep him waiting. Go at once, dear.

[*Exit* EVA C. D. *Pause.*

FER. I presume that I must introduce myself, as Miss Eva——

ART. (*Stiffly*). That ceremony will not be unnecessary. Whom have I the honour of receiving at Mompesson Abbey ?

FER. My name is John Ferne, civil engineer.

ART. Ferne! a relation of the Snobbses, no doubt. (*Aside.*)

FER. May I now inquire whom I have the honour of addressing ?

ART. Certainly ! Dr. Brown.

DR. W. N. Brown.—No final E.

ART. Mr. Bunnythorne.

BUN. Late of Bunnythorne and Bingham, contractors, Gosport.

ART. I am Mr. Arthur Mompesson.

BUN. The Honourable Arthur Mompesson.

DOC. What the devil's the Honourable to do with it ? A man's a man, isn't he?

BUN. Not invariably. Sometimes he's a gentleman.

ART. Not often. (*Aside.*)

BUN. He gave you your title of Doctor, didn't he ;—why not give him his title of Honourable?

DOC. My son wouldn't be a doctor, would he ?

BUN. What nonsense you talk—you haven't got a son.

DOC. There I have the advantage of you—you have.

ART. Chut ! chut ! Mr. Ferne, pray take a chair.

[*They all sit.*

| R. | | FERNE. | ARTHUR. | | L. |
| | DR. B. | | | BUNNYTHORNE. | |

Your name is not unfamiliar to me !

FER. My grandfather was a tenant on this estate, and I remember you, Mr. Arthur, as we called him, perfectly.

ART. (*Aside.*) A tenant ! (*Aloud.*) If I remember rightly, your grandfather had an old-fashioned name. Let me see— Jabez—Jabez, was it not ? (FERNE *assents.*)

Doc. Jabez Ferne! Any relation to the Jabez Ferne who patented the invention for drainage by means of——

Fer. His son! My father!

Doc. (*Rising and shaking hands with* FERNE.) He was an honour to science and his country.

Bux. (*Crossing, and shaking hands too.*) So he was, for we bought the patent, and sold it in the colonies to an enormous profit.

Doc. Profit! Think of making two blades of grass grow in place of one. Think of benefiting your fellow-man!

Bux. Think of benefiting yourself.

Art. May I inquire if you follow the same career of sewerage your father did? Do drains run in your family?

Doc. Drains don't! Brains do!

Fer. But then brains are not always hereditary. I have already told you I am an engineer.

Art. Pardon me! I had forgotten.

Fer. (*Aside.*) They're very disagreeable.

Art. An engineer! Well, engineers are the heroes of the hour—I should say of the minute—for the present age goes so fast that we have to count by minutes.

Fer. The present age is, certainly, the age of progress.

Art. Progress! Yes! That is the word. That is the modern slang for the destruction of everything high and noble, and the substitution of everything base and degrading. Progress! progress which pushes painting aside to make room for photography. But painting is old-fashioned; and photography—which makes men uglier than they are by nature—that's progress! Citric acid—and heaven knows what other abominations—have superseded grapes;—you literally *make* wine — that is science! Horses, which in my youth were considered noble animals, are abolished for engines that smash, for trains that smash, for velocipedes that smash; and the debris of broken wheels, boilers, bones, and shattered human beings, you call progress!

Bux. }
Doc. } Bravo! bravo! beautiful. (*Enthusiastically.*)

Art. As to manners, progress has indeed altered them. Every one is too much occupied to think, to feel, to love, or to improve. Progress does not permit sleep, or sentiment, or accomplishment, or leisure. To misquote Shakspeare—another illusion of my youth, and, doubtless, an impostor—"Whatever is done must be done quickly." Now-a-days you eat rapidly, you drink rapidly, you make love rapidly, you

marry rapidly, you go through the Divorce Court still more rapidly. Luxury everywhere; comfort nowhere. Look at your young men! cynical, sarcastic—without faith in anything; without warmth of heart, without generous enthusiasm—*blasé* and brutal—they puff the smoke of their foul cigars in the faces of their mothers, or swear before their sisters. Their talk is slang; their morals those of betting-men. Their aim to dazzle for a moment—their end bankruptcy of person, fortune, mind, heart, brain, body, and soul.

Bun. } (*Rising and shaking hands with Ar-* } *Together.* } Too
Doc. } *thur, then seating themselves again.*) }
true! too true! (*Shaking their heads.*)

Doc. The world is going to the devil.

Bun. At express speed (limited). And it used to be so good. We used to be so good! Didn't we, Doctor?

Bun. }
Doc. } We did!—we did! We used to be so good. Ah!
[*They sigh.*

Doc. These modern fellows, with their modern fashions, their beards and moustaches!

Bun. Too lazy to shave themselves. Hairy beasts!

Art. So un-English—pah!

Bun. And their floppy clothes, and their eyeglasses stuck so. (*Imitating.*) Ah!—ah!—ah!

Doc. And their cigars.

Bun. (*Imitating.*) Ah!—ah!—ah!

Doc. Ah! The good old times!

Bun. }
Doc. } (*Together.*) Ah! The good old times.

Doc. The men of old!

Art. Alfred! the Black Prince! the Fifth Henry!

Doc. Pooh!—Jack Cade—Cromwell!

Art. Pooh! Claverhouse—Marlborough!

Bun. Whittington, Lord Mayor of London!

Fer. Why not his cat?

Doc. Bacon!

Bun. Milton! Guy Fawkes! Mrs. Fry!

Doc. Thistlewood!

Art. Pitt!

Doc. Fox—Cobbett—Horne Tooke!

Art. Junius!

Bun. Cock-eyed Wilkes!

Doc. Walter Scott!

Art. Byron!

Bun. Old Parr! Where do you find such pills now? I mean, where do you find such men now?

Art. Where indeed?

Art.⎫
Doc.⎬ Ah! (*They shake their heads mournfully over the*
Bun.⎭ *bright past and degenerate present.*)

Fer. Do I understand the meaning of this combined attack to be because I, as an engineer, represent modern progress? If so, I accept the challenge. All that you have said is but to contrast the vices of the present with the virtues of the past. I cannot think that we are so bad as you would make us out. Vice is vice, no matter in what epoch it exists, and I readily admit that we are not as good as we should be. But, to combat your examples. We are guilty of moustaches; that, you say, is un-English. How about Shakspeare, and Bacon, and Sir Walter Raleigh? They wore beard and moustache, and they were somewhat of Englishmen. We smoke cigars. Johnson and Goldsmith smoked pipes. What difference? If we smoke more, we snuff less than our grandfathers. You have recalled the names of men dead for centuries, to ask me if I could show a parallel to them in this year of grace? Alfred, the Black Prince, Marlborough, and Pitt. Why not Pericles, Lycurgus, Alcibiades, or Solomon, or David, or Noah? For our manners, our cynicism, and lassitude, let it be remembered that we no longer beat watchmen, or steal knockers and bell-pulls for the sake of showing our wit. If we use slang, at least we are not guilty of the brutal oaths that, in the last century, made the name of Englishman a by-word over Europe. On one point, too, I must claim superiority even for our poor, weak, little modern selves—we keep sober. Men do not now reel into a drawing-room and bend over our mothers, wives, sisters, and daughters, to pump out compliments with a breath reeking of fiery port, with a faltering articulation, and unsteady step, and a tongue so loose and unguarded that it can scarce refrain from insult. From the usual degradation of daily drunkenness we are freer than our fathers, and——

Bun. (*Rising in indignant fury.*) Who the devil are you to turn up your nose at a man who gets drunk? Let me tell you, young sir, that I got drunk before you were born. Everybody got drunk before you were born. A parcel of stuck-up sober puppies! To get drunk properly and like a gentleman is a very good thing; it's—it's—it's English—

thoroughly English, and old-fashioned—and—and—all right! (*Sits down, blowing the steam off.*)

FER. You have sneered at this age because it is an age of progress; I prefer to call it a period of transition. We have changed from the worst to the better—we are changing still, from bad to best; and during this transition—I am proud to know that it is I—the engineer, the motive-power—who leads the way. 'Tis I who bring industry, invention, and capital together; 'tis I who introduce demand to supply. 'Tis I who give the word—'tis I who direct the train that flies over valleys, through mountains, across rivers—that dominates the mighty Alps themselves. 'Tis I—the engineer—who exchanges the wealth of one country against the poverty of another. I am broad, breathing humanity, that whirls through the air on wings of smoke to a brighter future. I spread civilization wherever I sit a-straddle of my steed of vapour, whom I guide with reins of iron and feed with flames. As for the tumble-down old ruins I knock down in passing, what matter? Where I halt towns rise, and cities spring up into being. 'Tis the train that is the master of the hour. As it moves it shrieks out to the dull ear of prejudice " Make room for me! I must pass and I will! and those who dare oppose my progress shall be crushed! " Its tail of smoke is like the plume of a field-marshal; and the rattle and motion of its wheels are as the throb and pulsations of the progress of the whole world.

ART. Possibly you are right, sir. (*Rising.*) Coal smoke is better than pure air;—the shriek of an engine is the sweetest harmony, and rapid motion is the sole secret of truth and happiness; but in my time it was not considered the act, I will not say of a gentleman, but of an honest man, to make signs to a young lady at a window, or to enter the house where she lived to speak to her clandestinely.

FER. What! (*Rising.*)

DOC. You have been observed, sir. (*Rising.*)

BUN. (*Rising.*) The whole morning—drawing, writing, and making signs at this window.

FER. To Eva?

ART. Eva! (*Aside.*) (*To* FERNE.) To Miss Mompesson, my cousin!

FER. I am compelled to contradict you most emphatically. Eva—Miss Mompesson—whom I met in London, called me in from that window. Until she did so, I was not aware that she lived here.

ART. Then why write?

24

FER. Write! I was not writing; I was sketching.

Doc. Sketching?

ART. In this weather?

FER. Yes, a bird's-eye view of this place and the neighbourhood, by order of the company of which I am chief engineer.

ART. Eh?

FER. Ses! (*Showing portfolio.*) We are going to make a branch line from Stapleton, through Broxborough and Wainthrope to Stickon-le-Clay.

Doc. ⎫
ART. ⎬ A railway here!
BUX. ⎭

FER. Yes. (*Showing drawing.*) Yes, here is the line; you see it cuts this park and the house in two——

Doc. ⎫
ART. ⎬ The Abbey?
BUX. ⎭

FER. Yes! The station will be built on this site. We must pull the Abbey down.

ART. Pull down the Abbey! Do I hear rightly? Pull down the Abbey! where my family for centuries have been born, lived, and died. Where I first saw the light; where, when my time shall come, I hope my eyes shall darken to this world, to open in a brighter and a purer. Pull down the Abbey! The royal gift of a king to my ancestor for faithful services in council and in field. A home where generations of knightly gentlemen and high-bred ladies have gone forth to rule the world and live in honour! A church, beneath whose aisles saints have spoken and martyrs have been buried. A holy shrine, reverenced by every passing peasant, where hospitality and every earthly charity, as every spiritual good were sanctified in stone. Pull down the Abbey! Sooner than see it trampled to dust and scattered to the winds, its stones shall fall and crush its master. (*Giving way, sinking into chair.*)

Doc. (*Going to him*). Arthur!

FER. I am very sorry——

ART. We fly their cursed civilization—their genius of smoke —their factory palaces—their spinning-jennies—printing-presses, and inventions of the devil. My father and I are not left even this retreat.

BUX. Here, here, here. This can soon be settled. (*Taking portfolio*). Look here; by letting the line diverge here, at the Park Gates, it comes round here, knocks down old

Brewster's new house, and there you are for your station; and any compliment that you may consider your due, for altering your plans, we shall be most happy to pay money down.

FER. (*Taking portfolio*). It only needed such a suggestion to recall me to a sense of my duty. I shall recommend this route. (*To* ARTHUR). At the same time I shall be glad, for your sake, Mr. Mompesson, if the Company, in considering the matter, should modify my instructions, and the Park and Abbey should remain intact.

ART. (*Rising*). You are right, sir; and I beg your pardon for having for a moment doubted you. I recognize you as a perfect man of honour, in your way—your rail-way; but I shall go to London—I will appeal against this invasion of my rights. (*During this last speech* EVA *enters* C.D., *overhearing the last words;* BOB *appears at* C.D.; MISS MYRNIE *at door* R.) I have friends, and powerful ones; I will see whether a Railway Company can uproot the home of a country gentleman. (*Music Piano till end of Act*).

EVA. You are going away, cousin?

ART. Yes; to London.

DOC. ⎫
BUN.   ⎬ (*Together*). To London!
MISS MYR. ⎪
BOB.   ⎭

    [*Picture.* FERNE *bowing to take his leave.* ARTHUR *indignant.* BUNNYTHORNE *and* DOCTOR *sympathetic.* EVA *looking at* FERNE. BOB *contemptuous.* MISS MYRNIE *watching.*

      MISS M.   BOB.
FERNE.   EVA. ARTHUR.   DR. B.   BUNNYTHORNE.

END OF ACT I.

ACT II.

Scene I.—*The Tapestry Chamber in the Abbey. Large Window,*
c. Balcony and staircase seen behind it—covered with snow.
Doors R. *and* L, 2 E. *Scene enclosed. Large old-fashioned*
fire-place R, 1 E. (*See Diagram.*) *Large fire burning. The*
stage furnished somewhat sparely. Old-fashioned tapestry on
walls. Table and invalid chair near fire-place. Sofa L.

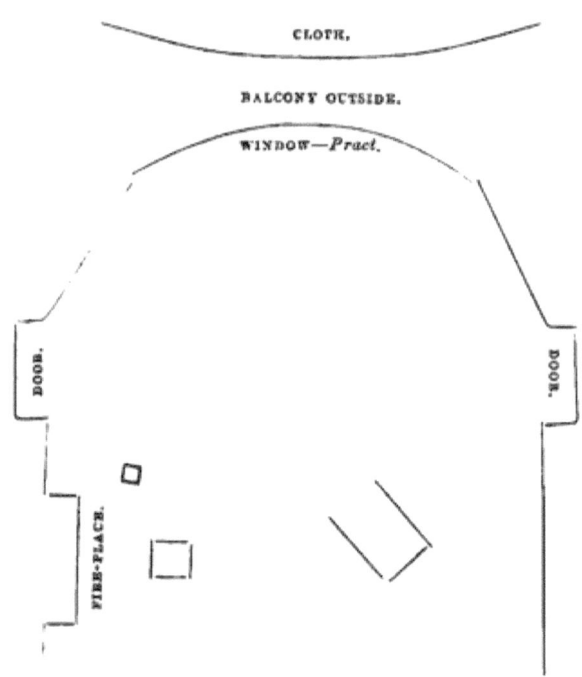

27

Enter DOCTOR *from door* R. (EVA'S *room*), *meeting*
WYKEHAM, *on whose arm* LORD MOMPESSON, *in dress-
ing gown, is leaning, who enters* L. D.

LORD M. Good morning, Doctor: good morning. How is
our invalid?

DOC. Much the same.

LORD M. Poor child! poor child! I miss her very much.
She was so kind and thoughtful for me—so kind and thought-
ful—so—so—Wykeham takes care of me now—don't you,
Wykeham?

WYK. Yes, my lord.

LORD M. But you're too old; ain't you, Wykeham—too
old?

WYK. Yes, my lord.

LORD M. So am I. In fact, we're both too old—ain't we,
Wykeham?

WYK. Yes, my lord.

LORD M. Do you think we shall have Arthur back to-day?
(*To* DOCTOR.)

DOC. I think so.

LORD M. Dear! dear! dear! And he thought to be only
away a week, and he has been more than two months—
such a long time—when one is old. Take me back to my
room, Wykeham. Let me know if Arthur comes back.

DOC. Of course.

LORD M. My love to Eva. Is she asleep?

DOC. Asleep? yes.

LORD M. Ay, ay! A good thing sleep. Good morning.
Now, Wykeham.

[LORD M. *and* WYKEHAM *totter off* L. D.

DOC. Asleep! ah! (*Sighing.*) If she only could sleep.

Enter EVA R. D. *She looks very ill, and half delirious.
During the scene she excites herself so as to exhibit
all the symptoms of delirious fever; she coughs at
intervals.*

DOC. Have you got up, dear?

EVA. Yes; don't scold me; I was so tired of the sick room.

DOC. (*With great sympathy, all his rough manner gone, and
the fine delicate nature rising to the surface.*) Feel better?

EVA. (*Languidly.*) Just the same.

DOC. And your head?

28

EVA. Heavy. And my bones all ache.

Doc. Sit down by the fire. (*Arranging pillows and arm-chair for her.*)

EVA. I'm always cold. My long illness began just in this way—but this time it will not last long.

Doc. Chut, chut! my dear. Come, you're more comfortable there.

EVA. I should like to be near the window.

Doc. The window is too far from the fire.

EVA. But I like to see——

Doc. There's nothing to see, my pet, but the snow that has fallen during the night.

EVA. I like to see the snow—the fantastic forms it seems to carve upon the trees—as if the whole world were made of white coral; or as if some good person were dead, and a shroud of ice had fallen upon the earth. Let me go to the window? (*Rising.*)

Doc. No, no; there is too much draught. It's a crazy old casement, and you mustn't catch cold. The slightest chill—an open door—or a current of air upon you in your state ——

EVA. And I should die?

Doc. (*Bothered.*) Die! No, my love: nobody dies! it's out of date.

EVA. But it *might* kill me!

Doc. Well, it might, if it were fatal. If you must move, walk about with me—so—within range of the fire. (*She rises, takes his arm, and they walk to and fro.*)

EVA. Tell me, is it true that there are people in the world who believe, that when we die, all is finished—all is over—and that we do not meet those we love again in a better, higher sphere?

Doc. I—I believe that there are such people. The world is full of varieties.

EVA. (*Growing delirious.*) But how is it possible they can believe it? How can they believe it—at night—when the sky is full of stars? What are the stars but beacon-fires of immortality? lamps, lighting us on the heavenly road to future and Eternal Life? Doctor, did you ever, on a bright night, see a star—fall?

Doc. Yes, often. I've seen many things fall at night.

EVA. And did you not think as you watched it out on its bright path, through its host of shining sisters, did you not think that *you* were that star—falling, falling, falling through tremendous, space—and have you not felt here, at your

heart, a sense of sublime emotion—a sort of wonder and awe, but yet not fear?

Doc. No; I never felt anything of the sort. We doctors, you know, have to deal with material ailments—broken collar-bones, and not erratic nebulæ.

Eva. I saw my mother die! When I die I shall meet her again! I shall cleave through the air and see the white frosty earth below me as I aspire to a bright heaven and her warm heart. She, above, cannot forget her poor child who, even in her earthly clay, remembers her. (*Coughs.*)

Doc. My child, you're feverish, go back to your room (*seating her in arm-chair*). Your head is hot, and——

Eva. Yes, I feel I am very ill, but I think that when the poor body is weak, the mind is clearer. (*Suddenly.*) Doctor, why do you never go to church?

Doc. (*Staggered.*) Eh?

Eva. Why do you never go to church?

Doc. Me—a—a man—at my time of life.

Eva. (*Slowly.*) If I were to die——

Doc. Eva!

Eva. If it were Heaven's will, and I should die, you would pray for me, would you not?

Doc. I—I—I—you really must go to bed, my child.

Eva. God bless you for all your goodness to me.

Doc. (*Awfully affected.*) My love! [*Music, piano.*

Eva. (*After a pause, taking* Doctor's *hand.*) They sent him away on my account; did they not?

Doc. Him? Who?

Eva. John—Ferne. You remember, I told you. They sent him away; Miss Myrnie told me so; because he was in love with me, and they did not think him good enough to be my husband.

Doc. Miss Myrnie told you so, did she?

Eva. Yes.

Doc. (*Aside.*) The damned old ——, I'll give her some physic that will make her so ill. (*To her, soothingly.*) My dear, Miss Myrnie told you a lie. So far from sending him away, your cousin Arthur likes him very much, and wishes him to marry you.

Eva. (*Overjoyed.*) What?

Doc. Miss Myrnie is a mischief-making old ——. With your permission, I will think the rest in Latin. Your cousin Arthur has gone to London——

Eva. (*Eagerly.*) To inquire about him?

30

Doc. Yes; yes. (*Aside.*) What an infernal liar I am; but it's a pious fraud. (*To her.*) And when he comes back——

Eva. He will be my husband?

Doc. Yes. (*She sinks into chair. A pause.*)

Eva. (*After a deep sigh of relief.*) Doctor, I think I'll go back to my room. I can sleep now.

Doc. Do, dear, do. (*She takes his arm.*)

Eva. Will he come soon to see me?

Doc. I—I think so; but how do I know? I'm not in his secrets.

Eva. (*As they are nearing door R. H.*) It's two months since I saw him; two months and three days.

Doc. Yes, dear, so it is. I make it out two be just two months and three days.

Eva. (*At door.*) Good night.

Doc. You mean good morning.

Eva. I shall sleep well, I'm sure I shall. (*Going, returns.*) If he comes while I'm asleep, you'll rouse me, will you not?

Doc. I'll come and rouse you up that instant.

Eva. Do. Oh! Doctor, why did you not tell me this good news before. I am so happy. [*Exit Eva. Door R.*

Doc. (*His handkerchief to his eyes.*) Poor child! poor child!

Enter Bunnythorne, *all over snow, L. D. Skates in his hand.*

Doc. (*Angrily and brusquely.*) What the devil do you come in like that for? Don't you know that I've got an invalid there? (Bunnythorne *is writhing in pain.*) What are you doing?

Bun. I'm trying to get my back-bone straight again. I've been skating on the lake.

Doc. More fool you—at your time of life.

Bun. And I tumbled down.

Doc. Of course—and hurt yourself?

Bun. Yes.

Doc. Where?

Bun. Where I fell—on my back.

Doc. Fall on your head next time, it won't hurt you there.

Bun. Arthur Mompesson's come back from London.

Doc. No! When?

Bun. This moment. Here he is.

31

Enter ARTHUR, L. D., *followed by* MISS MYRNIE. ARTHUR *is dressed in a modern morning suit, turn-down collar, modern cravat, &c., his whole manner changed, he seems younger and brighter, and radiant with high spirits.*

ART. Ah, Doctor, how d'ye do? Where is my father? Where is Eva?

DOC. Not yet up.

ART. Still asleep. (*Looking at watch*) and past ten. The lazy creatures.

DOC. (*With his watch.* BUN. *and* MISS M. *take out their watches, big ones.*) Past ten! Why it's not half-past nine.

ART. You're all slow here—behind time. Its past ten by the Horse Guards.

BUN. The Horse Guards at Stickton-le-Clay?

ART. No; the Horse Guards in London.

MISS M.　⎫
DOC.　　 ⎬ (*With contempt.*) Oh, London!
BUN.　　 ⎭

BUN. (*Dogmatically.*) Our time is Stickton-le-Clay time; that's good enough for us.

ART. Well, Doctor, congratulate me, I've won.

DOC. Won!

ART. Yes; I went to the Commons—the Lords—I saw many old friends—I argued—I fought—and conquered—the line is to branch off at Broxborough. Wainthorpe is to be left to the right, and the railway line does not come here.

MISS M. (*Rising and shaking hands with him.*) Bless you!

DOC.　⎫
BUN.　⎬ Hurray!

ART. (*Looking round with rapture.*) These dear old walls; I have preserved them! They will still stand—a glorious relic of past ages—an architectural beacon to the future. Progress, with its hot oil and steam vulgarity, shall not reach us here.

DOC.　⎫
BUN.　⎬ Bravo!

ARTHUR *standing with his back to the fire,* R. H., *the others seated.*

MISS M.　　　　DR. B.

ARTHUR　　　　　　　　　　BUN.

32

ART. But let us be just even to our enemies; the railway is very comfortable.

Doc. The railway? (*Astonished.*)

BUN. Did you travel by railway? (*Disgusted.*)

Miss M. Good gracious! (*Horrified.*)

ART. As far as Stapleton. (*All aghast.*) Why not? It was the nearest and the quickest.

Miss M. You travelled——

BUN. By rail? (*A pause.*)

ART. Yes, by rail; nice carriage—padded—tins full of hot water for your feet—very comfortable. When you stop at a station, man shouts out, Staple—ton, Staple—ton, bell, whistle, off you go—very nice indeed. (*They all sigh.*) I didn't care much for the coach—the old "Perseverance"—afterwards. Not pleasant inside. Commercial man asleep on my shoulder, a good snorer; woman opposite with baby with whom travelling disagreed. Damp, bad-smelling straw, the roads awful. Had to get out and walk up the hills. Cold, wet feet—after the comfortable first-class carriage. Horrible! (*A pause. DOCTOR, BUNNYTHORNE, and MISS MYRNIE exchange glances.*)

BUN. Where did you get those clothes?

ART. Oh! a tailor in Bond Street. I was so shabby. I ordered them and he sent them to Long's.

BUN. I never saw such an object in all my life. Why not wear moustaches?

Doc. And an eye-glass?.

Miss M. Or smoke a cigar?

ART. Ah! You're prejudiced! I've brought presents for all of you—and as for Eva. I've ordered fresh furniture for this room.

Miss M. Fresh furniture?

ART. Yes; I mean to make it into a boudoir. Poor child! after the luxury of London, to be condemned to pass her days among these mouldy old chairs and tables. They're only fit for an outhouse.

BUN. And what are we fit for? An outhouse too?

ART. My dear friends, my trip to London has made me twenty years younger. We'll make the old Abbey as gay as any place in the country. I mean to give a ball in honour of my victory over the railway.

Miss. M.)
Doc. } A ball!
BUN.)

BUN. Do you expect me to dance?

33

Miss M. Or me?

Art. Why not?

Miss M. Is the ball too to be in honour of Eva?

Art. Yes.

Miss M. Why not marry her?

Art. Why not?

Miss M. (*Rising.*) Balls, cousin Arthur, are wicked things —all sin and shoulders. If a ball is given in the Abbey I shall quit the place for ever.

Bun.}
Doc.} (*Together.*) Hurray! (*Congratulating each other.*)

Miss M. (*Hearing them, and more exasperated.*) I dare say you'll be very glad.

Bun. We shall, indeed.

Miss M. I will not countenance such scandals with my presence. (*Drops her spectacles.*) Cousin Arthur, the place of future punishment is paved with——

Doc. With good intentions.

Miss M. No, sir! with bare necks and shoulders, with false hair and paint, and other Babylonian abominations. Arthur, you went out from the country pure and unsullied. You have returned reeking with smoke, railways, impiety, and London. In time you will have ceased to be a single country gentleman, and sink into a married cockney! [*She goes off* L. D.

Bun. (*After a pause of astonishment, seeing her spectacles on the carpet.*) She's left her green spectacles. (*Crushes them with his foot, then picking up the pieces.*) Here, Miss Myrnie, you've dropped your spectacles. [*Exit* Bun. L. D.

Art. Upon my word, if Miss Myrnie were not——

Doc. Never mind the old woman—she's jealous.

Art. Jealous!

Doc. You said you'd ordered fresh furniture for Eva, and—

Art. Eva—yes—(*Looking at watch.*) Not up yet—lazy— I'll knock at her door. (*Going to door* R. Doctor *stops him.*)

Doc. No.

Art. Eh? Why not? (*Seeing the serious expression of* Doctor's *face,*) Is she ill? (Doctor *nods.*) Very ill? Why did you not tell me? Why did you not write?

Doc. What use? She fell ill two days after you left, and she has got worse and worse.

Art. Is it a return of—a relapse. (Doctor *nods.* Arthur *sinks into chair.*) But what cause?

Doc. What cause? (*Putting both hands in his pockets and looking* Arthur *full in the face.*) Love!

34

ART. Love! (*Rising, astonished.*)

Doc. Yes; for that young man—Ferne—the engineer.

ART. Impossible! He is not in love with her.

Doc. No; he is not in love with her, but she is in love with him.

ART. How do you know?

Doc. I heard her name him when she was delirious. (ARTHUR *resumes his seat.*) I questioned her, and she confessed it. She fell in love with him more than a year ago—when they were both in London. See here—(*Producing letter*), from the physician who attended her. (*Read.*)

ART. (*Reading.*) "If the fever returns in its full force, nothing can save her." (*Rising.*) But it shall not return. You are here. You can battle with the disease. You can save her!

Doc. Save her! How? Give me a body in pain, and I can try. Show me a diseased organ, and I know what I'm about. I can treat. I can reduce. I have something material to fight with. But a mind in trouble—a spirit diseased—a soul in agony—how can I treat that? I can't give her a dose of resignation or two tablespoonfuls of hope. I can't cure a love-sick girl, dying of love.

ART. But no girl ever died of love. You've told me so a thousand times.

Doc. And I was right. They don't die of love, but love brings on fever, and they die of that.

Enter BUNNYTHORNE *hastily,* L. D.

Doc. (*Angrily.*) How often am I to tell you to come in quietly.

BUN. (*Angrily.*) I shall come in as I like.

Doc. (*Pointing to door* R.) What, when——

BUN. (*Softly.*) Oh, I forgot. But I'm annoyed! That young fellow—that Stokineer—Engineer—what is it?

ART. Ferne?

BUN. Yes, Ferne—is downstairs in the drawing-room, and wants to see you. I told Wykeham to send him away.

Doc. You did?

BUN. Yes.

Doc. You fool!

BUN. (*Indignant.*) Doctor Brown!

Doc. Go down again—ask him to take a glass of sherry; be attentive, polite, and bring him upstairs here in ten minutes.

35

Bun. Upstairs ?⎫
Art. Here ? ⎬ *Both astonished.*
           ⎭

Bun. But I don't understand——

Doc. Of course you don't. I don't expect that of you. (*Forcing him off.*) Now go.

Bun. (*As he goes.*) Ask that stokineer fellow——

Doc. Yes.

BUNNYTHORNE *is forced off*, L. D.

Art. I don't understand——

Doc. Eva must see him. Miss Myrnie told her that Ferne was ordered from the house on her account, because you and your father would not consent to the match. His presence will contradict the old serpent.

Art. But she must not believe——

Doc. Let her believe what she likes, so long as I can but save her.

Art. But it will be a lie to——

Doc. Yes, it will be a lie. Consider the lie physic, and swallow it with or without a wry face—as you please; but swallow it.

Art. But to-morrow we shall be forced to undeceive her.

Doc. Let us save her for to-day. We can think of something else to-morrow.

Art. But I will not consent——

Doc. You must!—you shall! Damn it, sir! Who commands by the sick-bed side—you or me? Give me the chance of saving her. Don't tie my hands. I'll snatch her from death if I can.

Art. Death! (*Terrified.*)

Doc. Yes. Send this young man away, and I'll not answer for her life eight-and-forty hours.

Art. (*Despairingly.*) Let him come! Let him come! Only save her, and I'll turn radical! (*Shaking hands with* DOCTOR.)

Doc. Hush! (*Going to door* R.) I hear her moving—place the sofa here. (ARTHUR *moves sofa near fire.* EVA *opens door* R. ARTHUR *offers her his arm.*)

Art. My poor girl. I'm so sorry to see you ill again.

Eva. I'm so glad to see you back. (*Coughs. They place her on sofa.*)

Doc. Keep yourself well wrapped up--the slightest cold—the smallest draught—and the consequences might be serious.

Eva. What a long time you've been away.

36

Doc. Arthur has been busy. (*Motioning to* Arthur.) He has just been bothering me about a matter, which I fear you have hardly strength enough to talk of.

Eva. (*Trembling.*) About——

Doc. Yes—about that—about Mr. Ferne. (*During the Act,* Eva *coughs at frequent intervals.*)

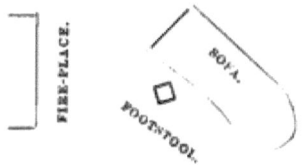

Eva. (*Trembling.*) Did you see him in London?

Doc. Yes; (*Looking at* Arthur.) You saw him in London?

Art. (*Embarrassed.*) Oh, yes.

Eva. Then you're not—your're not—angry—with him?

> Doctor *and* Arthur *are at back of sofa, so that* Eva *cannot see their by-play. The red light of fire on* Eva's *face.*

Doc. Angry with him—ha, ha! What for? (*Aside to* Arthur.) Say what for?

Art. (*Mechanically.*) What for?

Eva. For—for— Then Miss Myrnie was mistaken—and you did not——

Doc. No, you didn't, did you? (*Aside to* Arthur.) Say you didn't! I'm not going to tell all the lies—you tell your share!

Art. Did not what? (*To* Eva.)

Eva. You did not—decline his offer.

Doc. I should think not! (*To* Arthur.) Say no!

Art. (*Embarrassed.*) No!

Eva. Then you consent? (*She is almost fainting.* Doctor *applies eau-de-Cologne to her forehead.*)

Art. (*Taking* Doctor *up stage.*) What are you about? She believes that I consent to her marrying this fellow!

Doc. All the better.

Art. How can I undeceive her?

Doc. *Don't* undeceive her!

Art. You've done it, Doctor! You've done it!

Eva. (*Recovering*). What are you saying?

Doc. I was saying that Ferne is such a fine young fellow— make such a capital husband. He'll be here directly!

37

Eva. (*Excited.*) Directly!—When?—To-morrow?

Doc. When, Arthur? To-morrow; or, perhaps, sooner.

Eva. (*Sitting up on sofa.*) Hush! I hear his step! There are two people ascending the stairs; he is one of them. He is here! (*Sinks on sofa.*)

Enter BUNNYTHORNE *and* FERNE L. D.

Bun. (*Aloud.*) Here's Mr. Ferne. (*To* Doctor.) Now you've got him—what do you want with him?

Art. (*Going to* Ferne *and shaking hands with him with feigned cordiality.*) My dear Mr. Ferne—delighted to see you—delighted.

Doc. Delighted! (*Shaking hands.*) Delighted!

Bun. (*To* Ferne.) Eh! delighted? Why this is that fellow who was going to——

Art. ⎱ (*To* Bun.) Do hold your tongue!
Doc. ⎰ Keep quiet, can't you? [Bun. *bothered.*

Fer. (*Surprised at the warmth of his reception.*) I called partly to congratulate you on your success before the committee.

Doc. (*Interrupting him.*) And to inquire after Eva.

Fer. Eva!

All this takes place near L. H. *Door up stage.* Eva, *who is on sofa, not hearing it.*

Bun. Eva! (*To* Doctor *and* Arthur.) But I thought you didn't like the notion of——

Art. ⎱ (*Together.*) ⎰Do hold your tongue.
Doc. ⎰ ⎱Silence, you dreadful old magpie, silence.

Bun. (*Aside.*) They've both gone off their heads. London has sent one mad; and living among physic has driven the other lunatic.

Art. (*Aside to* Ferne.) For Heaven's sake, don't contradict a word we say.

Doc. (*Aside to* Ferne.) We'll explain to you by-and-by. (Ferne *astonished.*)

Art. (*Leading* Ferne *to sofa.*) She is very ill—very ill indeed.

Fer. I am very sorry, Miss Summers, to find you so suffering. So ill.

38

Eva. I have been ill, but I am better now.

Bun. (*Following* Doctor *and* Arthur. *To them, aside*) Now perhaps you'll tell me.

Doc. } Do keep quiet.   }
Art. } By-and-by, by-and-by. } *Together.*

Eva. And did you come down all the way here to see me?

Ferne. No. I came to see——

Doc. Yes; to see you, dear, of course—and Arthur—and all of us. (*Aside to* Bunnythorne). Say as I do—make much of him.

Bun. (*Mechanically crossing to* Ferne, *and shaking hands with him, quite bothered*). Yes, all of us—me particularly—always glad to see my dear friend, what's your name? Come often, and bring your steam-engine—I mean——

Eva. (*To* Ferne.) When you saw my cousin in London, he didn't know I was ill?

Fer. (*Mystified.*) When I saw——

Art. (*Interrupting.*) Yes, when we met in London. They never wrote and told me. (*Aside to* Ferne.) For heaven's sake don't betray us.

Doc. (*Aside to* Ferne.) It is life or death.

Art. We'll explain some other time.

Fer. (*To* Bunnythorne). Eh?

Bun. (*With importance*). Yes, I'll explain some other time, (*aside*) when I know what I've got to explain. (*Aloud*). By the way, lunch is ready—so if you, my dear friend, will lunch with us, I'm sure Mr. Mompesson will be——

Art. Delighted—yes, delighted.

Eva. No, you can lunch without him. He will stay with me. You're not hungry, are you? No; he is not hungry. Besides, I want to talk to him alone.

Bun. (*Astonished.*) }   }
Fer. (*Astonished.*) } Eh? } *Together.*

Doc. Yes. We'll go to lunch, and——

Art. (*Aside to him.*) Leave them together?

Doc. What is there to fear? He doesn't love her!

Art. No—but——

Doc. Do you want to murder her?

Art. No, no. There—there (*to them*)—I shan't be long.

Eva. Don't hurry on our account.

Art. (*To* Doctor.) We're done, doctor, we're decidedly done.   [*Exit* Arthur, l. d

39

Bun. (*To Doctor.*)   Now tell me why——

Doc. Don't bother now—only make much of him.

[*Exit Doctor, L. D.*

Bun. (*Bothered.*)   All right. (*Going to* Ferne *and shaking hands mechanically.*   Sorry you don't lunch with us, dear Mr.—— what's your name—but you must drop in some other time—drop in often—in a friendly way—devilish glad— (*goes off talking to himself,* L.D.)   [Ferne *astonished.*

Fer. What can they mean.

Eva. (*Smiling.*)   Well, won't you come and sit beside me.

Fer. With pleasure. (*Sits on sofa.* Eva *near fire.* Ferne L. *of her.*)

Eva. Oh! I am so glad to see you!

Fer. (*Embarrassed.*)   I, too, am delighted to have the opportunity. (*Formally.*)

Eva. And they never told you how ill I was—and I might have died——

Fer. Died! Oh, Eva.   How can you talk in that way.

Eva. You would have mourned me—would you not? (Ferne *embarrassed.*) But tell me—after you had seen cousin Arthur in London—why did you not write to me?

Fer. Write to you?

Eva. Yes; you knew the address!

Fer. (*Still more puzzled.*) Oh, yes; I knew the address.

Eva. Well, then.   Why not send me word of the good news immediately?

Fer. I—I hardly felt—justified.

Eva. Why not?   There was no need of any persuasion after cousin Arthur had given his consent.

Fer. Given his consent?

Eva. Yes.

Fer. To—to—what?

Eva. (*Blushing.*) To—you know very well—why do you want to make me say it?

Fer. Of course I know very well—but I should like to hear you say it, because then I might have an idea of what it was.

Eva. What a tyrant you are!

Fer. Do say it, Eva. (*Repeating.*)   Arthur Mompesson has given his consent——

Eva. To our—correspondence?

Fer. Correspondence!

40

Eva. Had given his consent—to our loving each other. There! now are you satisfied?

Fer. (*Aside.*) Good heavens! Does she love me?

Eva. So you could have written. Surely a man has the privilege of writing to his future wife.

Fer. Wife? Then have they told you——

Eva. The Doctor told me everything; so it is no use your trying to conceal it. (*Joyously—then sadly.*) I know why you and the others have tried to keep it from me.

Fer. Why?

Eva. Because I was so ill, they feared the emotion—the excitement of the news might kill me.

Fer. (*Aside.*) I understand.

Eva. But instead of increasing my malady it has improved my health. I feel stronger; I can breathe more easily. I can weep more freely. (*She weeps.*) Don't be frightened, these tears do me good. They are cool, refreshing tears— not like the hot scalding drops that burnt me yesterday.

> *During this scene the sky seen through the window becomes darker as if before a storm. At the same time the glow of the fire increases in colour on the faces of* Eva *and* Ferne.

Fer. But, Eva, if—if events should not have turned out so happily; that is, if I had not loved you, or if I had only loved you with the affection of a brother——

Eva. Oh! I shouldn't have liked that; that would not have been enough.

Fer. Or, if—mind I say if—if I had loved another.

Eva. (*Shaking her head confidently.*) Impossible!

Fer. Impossible! Why?

Eva. I loved you so much, you could not help loving me in return. These things are fostered by fate—or, no! I should not say fate, for mutual love is the work of Heaven.

Fer. Heaven! (*He rises and walks from sofa to* L. H. *Aside.*) I can hardly believe my senses. (*Returning to sofa and bending over her.*) And my love makes you happy, Eva?

Eva. Happy? Oh, infinitely!

Fer. (*With fervour, taking her hand.*) And I, too, dearest Eva, am happy.

Eva. Now sit down here, and tell me one thing. (*Ferne sits by her side again.*) Candidly, now—quite candidly.

Fer. Tell you what? (*This scene to be played slowly.*)

Eva. When did you first discover—that is, when did your heart first tell you that you loved me?

Fer. When?

Eva. Yes. When? (*A pause.*) Ah! you can't remember. That's like men. Now, I'll tell you when I loved you for the first time. (*With child-like confidence.*) It was on the twenty-eighth of September — on a Sunday. You called at the Dobbs's, and after dinner you walked out with me in the garden. It was the first time I had left the house since my illness. I was still in mourning, and you talked to me, and I fell in love with you from that moment.

Fer. (*With fervour.*) Yes—yes, I remember.

Eva. You remember what you said.

Fer. No, not exactly. (*Trying to remember.*)

Eva. I remember every word, because, you know, I was obliged to *guess* that you were in love with me.

Fer. Why?

Eva. Because you never told me.

Fer. Because I was a fool—absorbed in my idiotic business, and disregardful of the good, kind, warm, gentle heart that beat for me. I remember now your sweet looks, your pious resignation, your soft voice, and thousand charms. I observed them then, though not with the rapture I recall them now.

Eva. (*Entranced.*) Go on—go on. I love to hear you talk in this way. It is the first time your heart has declared its feeling to me.

Fer. (*His emotion mastering him.*) I remember all. I am again walking by your side in that glorious sunshine. Again I see your pale face looking into mine—I see your black dress —I feel your thin white hand upon my arm—I hear your voice —that voice that death had so nearly silenced for ever, but which returned to earth laden with music as of another sphere. I recall all—and the sunstroke that vivified my heart as your dear head rested there a moment—and the tears dimmed your eyes in memory of your mother. Eva, I loved you then, though I did not know it. I love you now, that you can be mine—my own, my partner through life—my wife for ever.

> During this speech Eva *has risen and stood by the side* of Ferne *as his speech reaches its climax, over-powered with emotion she falls unconscious on the sofa, at the same moment* Arthur *enters* L. D.

42

ART. (*Angrily.*) And I thought you were a man of honour.

FER. (*Not seeing that* EVA *has fainted.*) In what have I forfeited that title?

ART. In what? (*Seeing* EVA *unconscious.*) She has fainted. (*To* FERNE) Leave this house this instant.

FERNE. Leave this house! Who brought me into it, and welcomed me, and took me by the hand, and led me to hear her confession of love (*his tone rising with his words*), and to make my avowal of love to her?

ART. (*Violently.*) I order you to quit this house!

FER. (*Placing his finger on his lip to indicate that* EVA *might hear them*) (*scornfully*)—I obey your order; but I will return —return, despite of you, or all the world—to take away the bride I love—the wife who loves me—the woman to whom you have betrothed me! [*Exit* FERNE, L. D.

ART. Curses on the time I first saw you!—and oh! my punishment for taking the advice that brought him to her side! Eva!—still unconscious!

[*Going to bell-rope, sees* MISS MYRNIE, *who enters* L.D.

MISS M. What is the matter?

ART. Wait here with Eva, while I fetch the doctor. (*Crossing to* L. D.)

MISS M. (*Crossing to sofa.*) He's not in the dining-room!

ART. (*As he goes off* L. D.) I'll find him.

MISS M. (*Seating herself by* EVA's *side.*) Poor child! What a state they've put her into!

EVA. (*Recovering.*) Ah! How bright my future! How happy I feel! (*Seeing* MISS MYRNIE.) Miss Myrnie, where is he? He was here just now!

MISS M. Do you mean Mr. Ferne?

EVA. Yes. (*The sky becomes darker outside window.*)

MISS M. He's gone!

EVA. Gone!

MISS M. Yes; just this moment left the Abbey.

EVA. You are deceiving me, madam—deceiving me as you did before, when you told me that cousin Arthur would not permit our union.

MISS M. (*Enraged.*) I deceive you, my child! It is they who are deceiving you; I heard them during lunch. Mr. Ferne's love for you is all a pretence.

EVA. What?

MISS M. A plan—a scheme got up between them to comfort you because you are ill, and as soon as you are better they

will undeceive you. My poor child, I speak the truth; I never speak anything but truth.

Eva. His love a pretence—a plan!

Miss M. Yes, my poor child; they're treating you as if you were a baby, and I can't bear to see it, my sense of truth revolts at it; so I was resolved to tell you of it, that you might assert your sex's dignity.

Eva. (*Half convinced.*) And yet but now he told me that— he—loved me.

Miss M. He said that, my dear—out of pity for you.

Eva. (*Stricken.*) Pity!

Miss M. Yes, dear; the wretches to deceive you!—but I've unmasked them, and now you know the truth—the beautiful, the sublime, the glorious, the eternal truth!

Eva. (*After a pause.*) Please leave me, I wish to be alone.

Miss. M. (*Rising.*) Yes, dear; thank goodness I have done my duty. (*As she goes.*) To dare to insinuate that I could tell a lie. No! It's the men! Men are all liars! All! They lie to deceive us, but they have never deceived me, and they never shall! never! never! never! never!

[*Exit* Miss M. L. D.

The snow begins to fall outside window, at first slightly, then more thickly towards end of act.

Eva. (*After a pause.*) Pity! His pity! and all that he said as he sat here by my side. I remember. " If I had not loved you! " and, " If I had only loved you with the affection of a brother! " and " If I had loved another! " (*Rising from sofa.*) I see it all. He does not love me, and his bright words were lies. Oh! I am accursed! cursed like my poor dead mother! Why did I come here to this house from which she was banished—where I have been deceived? (*Coughs.*) Oh! air! air! (*Approaches window.*) I cannot breathe! No! (*Returning.*) I must not. The cold will kill me! (*Raising her head.*) Well, why not? Life is tasteless! Let me die!

Music—piano till end of act. She opens window and steps out into balcony amid the thick falling snow. Noise of wind heard as the casement is opened.

Eva *throws off the wrappings from her neck and shoulders so that she stands exposed to the snow in her petticoat body. She coughs frequently and places her hands on her chest.*

FERNE *appears on balcony, and as she faints catches her, and brings her into the room again. At the same moment* ARTHUR *and the* DOCTOR *enter* L. D. MISS M. *stands in* L. *door doorway. The* DOCTOR *rushes to window and closes it. Picture.*

DOCTOR at Window.

FERNE bending over her.   ARTHUR.

EVA on Floor.

Miss M. at Door.

Drop, Quickly.

END OF ACT II.

ACT III.

SCENE I.—*The same as* ACT 2. *Night. Stage dark. On table, near fire, bottle and tumblers, and sugar. Small copper kettle on fire.*

> *Enter* BUNNYTHORNE, *in dressing-gown and night-cap. He carries a lighted bed-candle in his hand. He is slightly intoxicated. Clock strikes five.*

BUN. Five! and that boy isn't home yet. I've been to his room, and there's his bed as smooth as a—brickbat. Oh, that boy! When I was a boy, what a charming boy I was!—innocent, ingenuous, good-tempered, brave, handsome, sober. I've taken too much brandy! The Doctor asked me to sit up in case he might want me, as Arthur is knocked up, and Miss Myrnie is in the dumps; and so I—brought the brandy—to rouse me—just to pass the time pleasantly—and then I fell asleep; and I suppose that in my sleep I—(*Growing maudlin sentimental.*) Poor child! poor child! (*Drinking neat brandy.*) Oh, that boy! (*He puts candle on table near sofa. The candlestick falls, and the light is extinguished. Stage dark.*) Confound it! In my time these sort of things never happened; but now-a-days—(*With disgust*)—Augh! (*He feels for candle; finds it; contemplates it moodily.*) Oh, that boy! (*Places candle in stick, and then places the candlestick on table, then feeling on floor.*) Luckily the lucifers were in the—ah! (*Finds lucifers on floor. During the following speech he strikes lucifers on box. They do not ignite. Irritably.*) Clever! (*Throwing lucifers away.*) Clever! clever! That's modern science! Only a penny a-box! But they don't light! (*Throwing lucifers away.*) Go it! (*Fondly.*) And when I remember in my time how pleasant it used to be with the dear old flint-and-steel and tinder-box, and those nice wooden matches, with the brimstone at the top—and you used to hit the steel on the flint, like a harmonious blacksmith—and after

the fifteenth or sixteenth stroke the spark would fall upon the tinder, and then the flames would spread about—"parson and clerk" we called 'em, in my innocent childhood—and then the match used to light—and ah! (*Sighing.*) The good old days! the good old days! (*A lucifer lights.*) Ah! at last! (*He lights candle. Stage light. Crossing stage to L. door.*) I wonder where the Doctor is! I'll go and see. (*As he reaches L. door, enter* BOB. *The draught from the door extinguishes the light. Stage dark again.*)

BUN. Oh, those boys! (*Angrily.*) Why did you open the door when you came in?

BOB. How could I come in without opening it?

> (BOB'S *boots and clothes give evidence that he has been walking in the snow. He is shivering with cold. He is partially intoxicated. To just the same extent as* BUNNYTHORNE. *His great coat and general appearance should resemble* BUNNYTHORNE'S *in his dressing-gown.*)

BUN. What d'ye mean by coming in at this time of night? —I mean morning?

BOB. I've been sitting up at the "Arms."

BUN. (*With disgust.*) The "Arms!"—a tavern? When I was a young man there were no taverns, and those there were closed early.

BOB. We were talking litera-too.

BUN. Talking what?

BOB. Litera-*ture.* (*With an effort.*)

BUN. (*Aside.*) The boy's drunk—drunk as a fidd-l-l-l-er!

BOB. (*Aside.*) The guv'nor's tight—tight as a drum.

> *Both assume an air of excessive sobriety and dignity.* BUN. *goes to sofa near fire.* BOB *follows him. As they cross, their resemblance to each other must be carried out by the actors' gestures and manners being arranged so as to be identical. Whatever action is used by* BUN. *is also used inadvertently and unconsciously by* BOB.

BUN. Why did you not go up to your room?

BOB. I wanted to inquire after poor cousin Eva! How is she?

BUN. I don't know—no better—just the same.

47

BOB. (*Spouting.*)

" She was doomed ere we were wedded, and I never saw her more.
Flame the lightnings, bray the thunders, bid the smoky torrents pour !
Bid the smoky torrents pour—— "

Oh ! smoky torrents—fine image isn't it ?

BUN. (*Not heeding him.*) Nothing to what it used to be in my time.

BOB. Eh ?

BUN. What's fine ?

BOB. My poetry—my " Thoughts in a Crater !"

BUN. Thoughts in a coal-hole ! I hate poetry—I consider it ungentlemanlike. There never used to be any poetry in my time.

BOB. (*Spouting.*) " Flame the lightnings—— "

BUN. Flame the devil ! Where are the lucifers ? On the table somewhere—find 'em. (*He finds them as he is speaking, and hands them to* BOB.) Here's the box—take it, can't you ? (*As* BUNNYTHORNE *holds box,* BOB *takes brandy bottle, helps himself, and drinks.*)

BUN. Got it ?

BOB. (*Drinking.*) Yes, I've got it.

BUN. You haven't—ah ! (*Lights lucifer.* BOB. *puts down glass.*) Hold the candle steady.

(*As* BOB *holds candle unsteadily,* BUNNYTHORNE *lights it also unsteadily. Stage light. They sit down again.*)

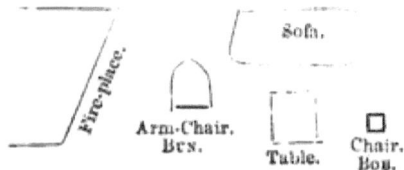

BOB. (*After looking at* BUNNYTHORNE.) Tight ! He's tight. (*Aside.*)

BUN. (*Aside.*) I'm sorry I didn't keep it dark.

(*During the scene, at intervals, they both endeavour to take the bottle at the same time, so that their hands meet, they withdraw them immediately, and endeavour to talk profoundly.*)

48

Bob. Do you know, governor, I'm getting tired of this sort of life ?

Bun. I should think so.

Bob. I feel I'm wasting my abilities, and the best years of my life in—in——

Bun. In getting drunk at the "Mompesson Arms."

Bob. No, governor, *I* am not drunk; but I know who is!

Bun. (*Indignant.*) Who is?

Bob. Never mind.

Bun. Who do you mean, sir?

Bob. Never mind—Jack Topham. (*Evading the question.*)

Bun. (*Sneering.*) Jack Topham—a pretty friend.

Bob. Oh! he's no friend of mine now—we've had a row.

Bun. Bravo! What about?

Bob. About Miss Brill, the barmaid; I think Jack's going to marry her. However, he cut up rough about her, and we had a row. (*Taking bottle.* Bunnythorne *stops him.*)

Bun. No; you've had enough already. Talking of Miss Brill, Bob, I used to be afraid that you were sweet upon her.

Bob. Me! no, governor. My mind is fixed upon Cousin Eva. (*Stage gets gradually lighter at c. window.*) And if it were not for this engineer ——

Bun. Those beastly railways! (*Amiably.*) Bob, my boy, I'd give the world to see you grow steady, and settle down with your cousin Eva.

Bob. (*Affectionately.*) Yes—guv—I should like to settle down. I've been stirred up enough already. (*Spouting.*)

> " For 'tis weary, weary, wasting mind and body at the oar,
> Rest thee—— "

Bun. Yes—Yes—Bob. I like you in your good humours.

Bob. Married to Eva. She'll have money.

Bun. Yes—yes. (*Aside.*) He is a good affectionate boy with all his faults.

Bob. And you'd allow me something if I was married.

Bun. Of course I would, Bob.

Bob. And with that capital I could go to London, and—start a new monthly magazine.

Bun. (*Horrified.*) What!

Bob. There is a great want of new monthly magazines in London, and I could publish my own poetry in it, and——

Bun. (*In a passion.*) You idiot — do you want to ruin me? (*Rising.*) You're no son of mine! I disown you. Ah! Get out!

soon. It's the only hope. Then there's Arthur. He's as hot-headed as a boy, and as obstinate as an old man. All the inconveniences of youth without its pliability, and the hardness of age without its obedience to the law of compromise. Here he is !

Enter ARTHUR, L. D.

ART. Well—what news ?

Doc. She sleeps—for the present.

ART. Tell me, candidly—candidly—will she recover ?

Doc. I don't know. (ARTHUR *sinks in chair.*) (*Aside.*) Now for it. (*Aloud*) I have no faith in my treatment—nor in anybody else's.

ART. Is there no hope ?

Doc. Yes, one.

ART. What is it ? (*Rising*).

Doc. Ferne.

ART. Ferne !

Doc. Don't fly at the mention of his name.

ART. He has killed her.

Doc. No ; 'tis you who will kill her by sending him away.

ART. Me ?

Doc. Yes. He, a plebian, has dared to fall in love with the niece of a Mompesson. Off with his head—eh ? Let the poor devil die of despair ; but no Mompesson must make a *mésalliance*, particularly with a rival——

ART. A rival ?

Doc. Yes ; a rival. I repeat it—rival ! If you havn't yet confessed it to yourself, learn it from me ; you've dream't of making this dear cousin your wife—of refurnishing the abbey, of the comforts, the joys of domesticity.

ART. (*Indignant.*) Doctor !

Doc. Ah ! I've found the wound then. Confess you are jealous !

ART. No ! (*Loudly.*)

Doc. Ah ! ah ! On your honour—on your honour ?

ART. Oh ! you're the devil !

Doc. I wish I was ! For if I were, I'd bribe you to do what's right, by giving you the youth (*with intention*), the appearance, and the attractions you possessed thirty years ago.

ART. But let us seek other advice—the London doctor who attended her during her last illness.

51

Doc. (*His hands in his pocket.*) I'd give the world to consult with him.

Art. I'll write to him.

Doc. Your letter will not reach London until to-morrow evening.

Art. I'll send—I'll go myself!

Doc. There's no railway nearer than Stapleton, and that's eight hours from here.

Art. We'll telegraph!

Doc. No telegraph nearer than Stapleton.

Art. (*Crossing to* R.) No rail!—no telegraph!—no anything in this damned hole! We're in a desert, and miles away there are contrivances that annihilate time and space. (*Stopping with sudden conviction.*) And it was I who crushed the project that would have brought communication with the world up to this very spot. (*Bitterly.*) Congratulate me on my victory! I have saved the Abbey, and I have killed Eva!

Doc. (*Aside.*) At last! (*Aloud.*) You see then this young man's calling has its noble, as well as its common tradesman side. Science commands time and space. King Canute couldn't command the tide, but the engineer can build a breakwater that compels the roaring ocean to keep within its proper bounds!

Art. But of what use is all this?

Doc. Of every use. Ferne is not, I will say, a man of good family. Well, he'll found a family, for he is a young and already distinguished man. He has that natural patent that is the commencement of distinction and nobility.

Art. And what may that be?

Doc. Brains—that coronet worn inside the skull, that no revolution can deprive him of.

Art. But do I understand that you wish me to——

Doc. To give her up to this young man? Yes, I do.

Art. (*After a pause.*) You are asking me to make a sacrifice —to exhibit a heroism which——

Doc. Of course I'm asking a heroism—a self-sacrifice. What else should I ask of you? Now take it from your own point of view, not mine. I'm a republican—a radical—in modern slang, a Red. I want to see some of this real nobility I hear you talk of. I want to see it, out of a picture, or a genealogical chart. I want to see it framed in flesh and blood. In this sad business I don't ask you to act like a common man; I don't ask you to act like a gentleman—that's easy to you—you

can't help it. I ask you to act like a Mompesson! Do you remember some time ago, in the year fourteen hundred and something, how your ancestor Raoul de Mompesson took service in Germany, and when the Archduchess Something-or-other-stein, with whom Raoul was in love, was pursued with her husband and children, by her enemies, your ancestor put on the Archduke's armour and alone met the foemen, who mistook him for his rival, and he fell pierced by their swords, and while he held the hilts of their blades to him the woman he loved gained the castle in safety; and, don't you remember, how she and the children he had saved offered up prayers for the chivalric lover who had died so true a knight, a gentleman, and soldier? Well, then, Raoul de—I mean Arthur de Mompesson, remember your race, your blood, your antecedents. Cast all small selfishness aside, receive this young man. Give up Eva! Save her life! Honour commands! Humanity insists. *Noblesse oblige!*

ART. (*After a pause, rising.*) You are right. Send for Mr. Ferne. I'll do it.

Doc. You will?

ART. (*Extending his hand.*) Upon my honour.

Doc. (*Shaking hand.*) Mompesson, all over. Raoul redivivus! (*And chuckling at his success.*) There's always some good in a gentleman, even when he's a nobleman!

[*Knock at* L. D.

(*Aloud.*) Doubtless that's him.

ART. Ferne? (*Doctor nods.*) Already? (*Mastering himself.*) Come in!

FERNE *opens* L. D., *and appears on threshold. He does not advance into room.*

FER. (*After a pause.*) Pardon me. I received a note from Doctor Brown, which——

ART. (*Offering his hand.*) Mr. Ferne, I have to ask your pardon for what I said yesterday. I was wrong, violent, unjust. I trust that you will accept my apology.

FER. (*Hardly comprehending.*) Mr. Mompesson, I——

ART. We must talk seriously. Will you sit down?

Doc. (*Aside to* ARTHUR.) Bravo!

FER. My position here is so peculiar. But I hardly know how I should act.

ART. There is, I admit, a difficulty; but no difficulty that cannot be overcome.

[*During* ARTHUR'S *last lines* EVA *enters* R. D.

53

Eva. (*At door.*) There need be no difficulty; or if there be. it is one in which I am concerned and have a right to speak.

Art. Eva! (*Advancing to her.*)

Doc. Hush! Leave them alone.

Arthur *and* Doctor *retire to window.* Eva *advances to sofa.* Ferne *approaches her.*

Eva. Mr. Ferne, let me be candid. Yesterday you told me that you loved me.

Fer. And I spoke the truth.

Eva. No. You saw me ill—as you thought dying—and you spoke from pity. I cannot accept your love as alms.

Fer. Alms!

Eva. I should have been proud of your affection, I must decline your compassion.

Art. (*Aside*). She rejects him. She is a Mompesson. (*With pride*).

Doc. (*Aside, at back*). Wait a bit. All the Mompessons on the female side were women, and women are fondest of their sweethearts when they quarrel with them. " It is their nature to."

Eva. You and my cousin, and the Doctor, and the rest of my kind friends, have treated me as if I were a child, and——

Fer. Eva, will you hear the truth—the honest truth—the truth that a man should tell to the woman he loves—the woman he hopes to share his life with? I came here absorbed with the small cares of the outer world—unthinking of you. I saw you—and the love that I had never dreamt of—leaped up at my heart. I remembered the old days in London, when I saw you as I see you now, pale—weak—beautiful—and a new feeling came over me. The love I feel for you throngs my veins, and I speak as I think when alone, and you are not near to dazzle me, and make me forget all but the sweet intoxication of your presence. Eva, I have the consent of your cousin, I dare to believe I have the consent of your own heart : you love me—your own sweet lips have avowed it. I love you, wholly, solely, and truly. Do you believe me ?

Art. (*Advancing.*) Yes, I believe him, and you may.

Eva. Are you sure you speak the truth ?

Fer. Let your heart answer for mine. My lips are silent.

Eva. (*After a pause, giving him her hand.*) Yes, I believe you !

54

Art. It's all over, Doctor. It's all over. What shall I do?

Doc. Do! congratulate them! (*Advancing.*)

Eva. But Miss Myrnie told me ——

[*Miss Myrnie appears at* l. d.

Doc. Miss Myrnie is a deceitful old—but no—why should I libel a harmless, necessary cat, by comparing it to a spiteful unnecessary old woman? Miss Myrnie ——

Miss M. (*Advancing.*) Miss Myrnie has heard every word, and Miss Myrnie does not think it necessary to defend either what she said to Miss Summers yesterday, or what she has said to Lord Mompesson this morning. Miss Myrnie has done her duty to her own conscience, to her religion, and to her family. (*Speaking at door.*) Your lordship will find every word that I have told you to be true.

Doc. Lord Mompesson! } *Together.*
Art. My father! }

Doc. The old devil.

Enter Lord Mompesson, l. d.

Art. (*Speaking to* Doc. *as* Lord M. *enters, and takes a chair,* c.) He will never consent. I know his prejudices. Now all is over!

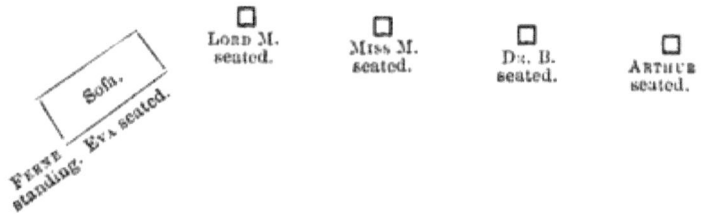

Lord M. Arthur—Eva—Miss Myrnie has been telling me of something that has been kept a secret from me.

Art. Only since yesterday.

Miss M. I have told his lordship everything.

Doc. (*Aside.*) And a little over. The truth made piquante with Miss Myrnie's sauce.

Lord M. Eva, my grand-niece, is it true that you have received the attentions of a young gentleman?

Eva. Of Mr. Ferne,—quite true. (*Rising.*) Mr. Ferne, let me present you to my grand-uncle, Lord Mompesson.

[*They bow, &c.*

55

Doc. (*Aside.*) Bravo!

LORD M. And Doctor, is it true that in order not to contradict Eva's whims or wishes while she was so critically ill, that you and Arthur told her that Mr. Ferne might visit the Abbey as her accepted suitor?

ART. }
Doc. } Quite true. (*Together.*)

MISS M. As I told your lordship, they trumped up a story—

LORD M. (*Interrupting.*) One moment, dear Miss Myrnie. Mr. Ferne, you told me, was not exactly a—a man of family.

MISS M. No family whatever! No blood, that is, no real blood. His veins are plebeian as potato peelings. He is connected with the railroads. I believe he is a railway guard, and his grandfather was a labourer on your lordship's estate.

FER. Permit me to correct you? I am an engineer. My grandfather held the Branxley Farm, close to Woodside.

MISS M. A mere question of detail.

LORD M. Aye!—aye!—aye! Ferne. I remember.

FER. If I may be allowed to offer a remark, I would suggest that I was asked here, and that I offer marriage to your niece, Lord Mompesson; that I do so from myself, and with no doubt of my own worthiness. I court inquiry as to my character and circumstances.

MISS M. Such impudence!

LORD M. Is my niece attached to you?

EVA. Let me answer that! I am!

MISS M. Well, if ever! (*Scandalized.*)

Doc. It's so many years since she felt anything of the sort she has forgotten all about it!

ART. My father will never consent. We're done, Doctor, we're done! (*To* DOCTOR.)

LORD M. Have you many relations, Mr. Ferne?

FER. None! I am alone in the world!

Doc. Oh! he's much too good a fellow to have relations!

LORD M. (*Rising and going to* ARTHUR.) Arthur, what is your opinion?

ART (*The* DOCTOR's *eyes fixed upon him.*) They are worthy of each other.

LORD M. And you would have me consent?

ART. Yes!

LORD M. Mr. Ferne, Miss Myrnie has done us all a great service in facilitating our meeting, and understanding each other on this very serious subject. I must inquire into many details. We need not enter upon that now. In the mean-

time, and until we know more of you—which I make a con-
dition—visit the Abbey in the capacity of my dear grand-
niece's suitor. I am an old man. I shall not be here much
longer. I would not see her mother after her marriage
(*mournfully*), and I never set eyes on her again. Let me
make those about me as happy as I can. (EVA *takes* LORD
MOMPESSON'S *hand*.) Dear Miss Myrnie here, I am sure, will
be pleased that her kind intervention has had so happy a re-
sult. (MISS MYRNIE *astonished*.)

DOC. Dear Miss Myrnie, I congratulate you.

FER. How can I find words to thank you? (*Crossing to her*).

EVA. (*To* MISS MYRNIE). And I was foolish enough to think
that you were not my friend. Thanks !

FER. Thanks !

LORD M. Thanks !

DOC. Thanks !   [*All to* MISS MYRNIE.

MISS M. (*Speechless with rage, masters herself*). Don't mention it—you're quite welcome. I—I will retire to my room.

DOC. Do—do! and don't come out again! (DOCTOR *opens
door*.)

[*Enter* BUNNYTHORNE *in coat and hat, followed by* BOB.
BOB *has a green shade over both eyes*.

MISS M. Good gracious! (*Seeing* BOB).

DOC. What's all this?

BUN. (*Leading* BOB *to chair*). Bob's been having a tooth out.
Topham on the eyes—but he licked him—I saw the fight—
Bob licked him. (*With pride*). The very image of me when
I was his age. When Eva gets better he's the husband for her.

MISS M. at window.

FERNE.   EVA.   LORD M.
seated.   seated.

DR.   BUN.

BOB.
seated.

BOB.

"In the rapture of the battle, when whirls wild the foeman's glaive,
Shall thy image aye be present to the bosom of the brave."

MISS M. (*Coming down to* BUN.) Miss Eva is engaged to
Mr. Ferne by my lord's consent.

BOB. What !

57

Bun. Bob!

Bob. Never mind, guv'nor; the brave heart accepts its doom. You can make me the allowance all the same. (*Re-seating himself moonily.*)

"Though I loved her, yet she left me—it is years and years ago;
  Once my eyes were dimmed with weeping, now my locks are white as
    snow."

Bun. (*To* Doctor.) I should like to know why——

Doc. Not now—some other time.

Lord M. (*As if concluding a conversation.*) Yes—yes—yes. And if all turns out satisfactory, of which I have no doubt——

Art. I will give the bride away.

Miss M. (*Sneering.*) With all your differences of opinion you seem quite agreed on one point, that Miss Eva must be married.

Doc. Yes, we're all agreed on that. (*Pointing to* Arthur.) Aristocrat.

Art. (*Smiling and pointing to* Doctor.) Red Republican.

Doc. (*Pointing to* Bunnythorne.) Man of business.

Bun. (*Leaning over* Bob.) And warrior!

Doc. Lords!

Bun. (*Pointing to himself.*) Commons!

Doc. (*Pointing to himself.*) The people!

Bun. (*Pointing to* Bob.) And the army!

Doc. Very good! Let's try again! High! (*To* Arthur.) (*Pointing to himself.*) Low! (*Indicating* Bunnythorne.) Jack!

Bun. (*Pointing to* Bob's *black eye, and slapping him on the shoulder.*) And Game! (*Crosses to fire-place.*)

Doc. Come, my patient, no more excitement to-day, or it will be too much for you. Let me take you to your room? (*Crossing to her.*)

[*Music, piano, during* Eva's *speech.*

Eva. A few minutes more to thank you; so much for all your goodness to me. I shall get better; I feel I shall! When the snow melts from the grass, I shall be stronger; and when the summer covers those black branches with green leaves I shall be able to walk down the avenue.

Fer. With me by your side?

Lord M. You, on one side—me on the other. Left to your-self your pace would be too fast, and mine would be too slow. You have youth, strength, and speed; I have age, judgment, and experience. Let Eva walk between us.

58

Eva. (*As they are going round door* R.) My path must lead
to happiness when love and hope conduct me, and affection
and experience guide me—(*Smiling.*)—That's progress!
          [*Movement of all the characters. Music ceases.*

Ferne.	Eva. Lord M. going to door.	Arthur. Dr. congratulating each other and seated.	Miss M. at door, disgusted.
Bux. seated.			Bon seated.

Bux. Now, in my time, we should have all stood in a pleasant half-circle round the stage, and thanked our friends, the
public, for their kind applause; but nothing is as it should be
now-a-days, everything is going to the——

Curtain quickly.